Having previously worked as a banker, Mark Neilson went on to become an Economics lecturer at Strathclyde University. He later became a consultant, but is now a full-time writer.

ANOTHER CHANCE, ANOTHER LIFE

In a cruel yet comforting parallel, friends Becky and Kathy have recently both lost their jobs, and face the prospect of starting their lives all over again. Taking up the offer to borrow her elderly uncle's narrow-boat, Becky sets sail for the Yorkshire Dales with her son Jonathon, wondering if new pastures might help her regain what she's lost. Meanwhile, Kathy finds herself in love with a widower whose only daughter is still in mourning for her lost mother — her grief proving a solid opponent to any new woman in her father's life . . .

Books by Mark Neilson
Published by Ulverscroft:

THE VALLEY OF THE VINES
A STRANGE INHERITANCE

MARK NEILSON

ANOTHER CHANCE, ANOTHER LIFE

Complete and Unabridged

ULVERSCROFT
Leicester

First published in Great Britain in 2015 by
Robert Hale Limited
London

First Large Print Edition
published 2016
by arrangement with
Robert Hale Limited
London

The moral right of the author has been asserted

A catalogue record for this book is available
from the British Library.

ISBN 978–1–4448–2724–8

Published by
F. A. Thorpe (Publishing)
Anstey, Leicestershire

Set by Words & Graphics Ltd.
Anstey, Leicestershire
Printed and bound in Great Britain by
T. J. International Ltd., Padstow, Cornwall

This book is printed on acid-free paper

1

Rebecca Calderwood quietly closed her front door, then leaned her back against it, looking as if she was taking refuge there from hordes of pursuers. The coldness of the glass struck through to her back and arms.

She refused to cry: crying solved nothing. Here, in the quiet sanctuary of her home, she would somehow find a way out of the catastrophe which had broken over her at the end of autumn term, and which was threatening to destroy everything she had built.

'Mum?' The boy's voice came uncertainly into the hall.

'Jon?' Becky's eyes snapped open. 'What are you doing home, at this time of day?' Three swift strides took her down the hallway and into their lounge, where the drawn and heavy curtains left barely any light. Her hand groped for, found the light switch. She blinked in the glare.

'Oh, no!' she whispered.

Her son was huddled in an armchair looking even smaller and more vulnerable than he was. Her eyes took in the dribble of blood smeared and caked beneath a nostril. The skinned knee. The scuffed shoulder bag, lying at his feet.

'Not again?' she said, sagging wearily against the door frame.

Her mind rebelled against the thought of taking on someone else's problems, when she was barely able to cope with her own. But this was her son, and he had no one else to turn to.

'Your dinner money? Did they take that too?' she asked.

His face crumpled. Suddenly, they were in each other's arms. She gently held his body, feeling the sobs which were tearing him apart. 'Shoosh,' she crooned, rocking back and forwards. 'Shoosh!' The old comforting Scottish word came instinctively to her tongue. His sobs gradually subsided.

'I'm not going back there,' he said mutinously.

'OK,' she said. 'Let's take a time-out . . . I think we both need it. Have you eaten anything since breakfast?' She felt his head shake. 'Right. How about some cordon bleu scrambled eggs? No? Cordon bleu beans on toast? You be chef, I'll set the kitchen table . . . '

She gently steered him to the bathroom. 'First, let's get that face clean — your nose stopped bleeding, ages ago.' She turned the hot tap on, let it run while she gathered some cotton swabs. She was getting expert at this — too expert. Even in a quiet school in Southport, bullies lurked, waiting for someone who was scared and smaller than themselves. After their marriage had finally collapsed, and Bob had left them behind, Jonathon had retreated into uncertainty, then fear. It had hurt, being abandoned; then hurt even worse, when her child was abandoned too.

She itched to confront the bullies but that wasn't how to handle it. She had been to the head teacher at his school, several times. They seemed powerless to stamp it out. The group of lads hung together and pleaded innocence, while everybody else made sure they didn't see anything — making it Jon's word against theirs.

'Why are you back so early, Mum?' he asked.

She gently dried his face. 'I've been sort of beaten up too. Been out looking for work, and got nowhere. I need care and attention. Get on that apron, and cook me up a storm.'

He grinned, mercurial as any small boy. 'Right, Mum,' he said.

Becky didn't want to eat. She had no appetite, no idea where to turn, what to do. After her marriage crumbled, she had taken her teacher training — only to lose her first job at Christmas — a victim of the education cuts. January and most of February had passed, without even making an interview. Her minor savings were almost exhausted. How was she going to keep up the mortgage payments on their flat? How long would the bank give her, to find another job? Would their home be repossessed?

She stared blindly at the place settings, listening to Jonathon clattering behind her at the cooker. She needed to talk this over with someone she trusted — and who better than the close friend she had made at teacher training? She would phone Kathy and arrange to meet her somewhere for a coffee and a chat.

They had plenty of time to meet, and plenty to talk about — they had been released within minutes of each other by the same embarrassed head teacher. But that's what friends were for, to lean on when things got tough. And it couldn't get much tougher than this, surely?

'What were you working on today, Jon?' she asked.

Frowning with concentration as he stirred the beans to stop them from sticking to the pot, he told her. Either he wasn't making sense, or she wasn't listening. His words simply didn't register. No matter.

'Show me, after lunch,' she said. 'Then I'll take you through it myself, this afternoon.' Once a teacher, always a teacher.

Even when you hadn't a classroom any more.

★   ★   ★

'OK, so we lost our jobs,' Kathy said defiantly. 'That's not the end of the world — things could be worse . . . '

'How?' Becky asked wryly.

Kathy's brown eyes twinkled. 'Well, maybe a tsunami could sweep away Southport pier . . . or aliens might take over Pleasure-land . . . '

'Would we notice any difference?' Becky smiled, her spirits lifting, responding to the energy and resilience of the younger woman.

They were sitting in a coffee shop known only to locals, well away from the funparks and the shopping arcade. It made the best coffee in town, and home baking to die for. A State of Emergency had been declared, all diets suspended, and the two girls had each indulged themselves in a cream cake.

Katie licked her fingers. 'There was nothing personal in losing our jobs,' she said. 'It happens to lots of people. We were the last two teachers in, so the first two to go. The head told us that she would have kept us both, if she had the choice. But she hadn't. So we simply make a fresh start on the rest of our lives.'

'Yes, but how?' asked Becky. 'I've been drawing blanks, for weeks.'

'Too soon to get worried. January is always the silly season, where nobody has really settled back to work and February isn't much better. I've been holding off looking, up until now — it's a waste of time. There has to be something out there, for us! Two young and gorgeous women . . . well, one gorgeous and the other not too bad.'

'So I'm 'not too bad'?' demanded Becky, taking mock offence.

Kathy blinked. 'Actually, I had you down for gorgeous. I was the other.'

'You're joking?'

'I run forty miles a week, and you're every bit as slim. If I look half as good as you when I'm forty . . . '

'I'm only thirty-three!' Becky exclaimed.

Kathy grinned. 'That's better! Come out of your corner, fighting.'

'So we look for new jobs. Does that mean we buy the same newspapers, and apply for the same posts? Then sit at opposite sides of the interview room, and pretend we don't know each other?'

'No way!' said Kathy. 'We sit together, while I try to think up a way to ladder your tights, or smudge your lipstick, before you go in for interview.'

Becky laughed out loud. 'Seriously, Kathy. How do we find work?'

Kathy chased crumbs round her plate. 'Actually, you've given me a good wake-up call. I've been drifting, waiting to start. I'm going to go home, put on my trainers, and go for a long hard run. That's when I think best. Let's both decide what we would most like to do with our lives, then meet on Thursday for a brainstorming session on what we need to do to achieve that.'

'I can't wait to start,' said Becky.

'Meanwhile, what are you doing this afternoon?'

'Catching a bus out to the convalescent home in Ormskirk, to see my old uncle Noel.'

'Convalescent? Is he . . . *senile?*'

Becky smiled. 'No. Nothing like that. He lost my aunt Ella about three years ago, and turned in on himself. Such a shame. When I was young, he was an overseas reporter for one of the big London dailies. He was like a cat — whatever happened to him, he always landed on his feet. Until Ella died, I didn't even think of him as old. But he's been neglecting himself, not eating properly. So I've been going over once a week, cooking a proper meal. And he's so stubborn! Last week he climbed a ladder to clear leaves from his gutter — then fell off. Cut his head — it needed stitches. The hospital saw how thin he was, and sent him to a convalescent home, to be assessed. He hates it there — and has gone into the huff.'

'Shame,' Kathy said quietly. 'A duty visit?'

'Anything but! Since my father died, he's been a father-substitute. When I was a kid, he was fantastic to visit, full of stories about what was going on in the world. I wanted to be an overseas reporter too. He used to take me places in his car, or their narrowboat, then make me sit down and write 500 words about what I'd seen . . . pruning it down to journalistic basics.'

'A narrowboat?' asked Kathy.

'My aunt and he used to disappear into the canal system for weeks, even months on end. They were like gypsies. Two inseparable people, poles apart in everything but their love for each other. Wherever they were, there was always fun and laughter. Never was any question of duty visits. In fact, I used to kick and scream, when my mum tried to drag me home.'

'He sounds a real character.'

'He was — and is. But when Ella went, she took all the sunshine from his world.'

Kathy stood up. 'I'm off. I've got a date with my running gear, to burn off that cream bun. I want to run out to Martin Mere, before the rush hour starts — fancy coming?'

Becky smiled. 'The only running I do these days is to catch a bus.'

'I could put you in a supermarket trolley, and push you in front of me?'

'Save that for Guy Fawkes Night,' Becky laughed.

The two women embraced, and Becky watched her friend stride off, with the easy co-ordination of a born athlete. For the four years she had known her, almost since the marriage break-up, Kathy had exuded an appetite for life and boundless enthusiasm. Which had made her a natural teacher, even if that was no longer an option.

Becky picked up the tab and searched through her bag for her purse. This coffee was a luxury she should have done without; but the contact with her younger friend, tapping into her strength and energy, had been priceless.

She walked to the cash desk. Trust Kathy, to see the way ahead. Losing your job wasn't the end of everything. It was the start of the rest of your life.

'Can I see you in here for a moment, Miss Calderwood?'

Becky turned, in the gloom of the hallway. It was the nursing sister, beckoning from the office door. She stepped inside, and the sister quietly closed the door, waving Becky over to the plastic chair on the far side of the office desk.

'Oh dear,' sighed Becky. 'Has Noel got himself into trouble?'

'Not yet . . . ' The sister's smile was wry. 'No, I just wanted to talk to you briefly. Mr Medwin's a lovely old gentleman . . . '

'But . . . ?'

The sister sighed. 'This huff he's taken at the world in general, is the start of a slippery slope. He's cutting himself off from the other patients, from staff, and drifting into a world of his own.' She studied her reddened nurse's hands. 'That's dangerous — we need to nip it in the bud. I hear warning bells when an independent person gradually loses interest in what's going on around him.'

'Would it help if you sent him home?'

'Quite possibly — but we can't really take the risk of letting him out. Would he pick up again — or would the recent pattern of self-neglect continue, when he has no help?

10

We have to balance the risks.'

The electric clock's minute hand jumped forward, startling Becky. 'I hear you,' she said uneasily. 'I feel so guilty about this. I would do just about anything, to help him recover, but I've lost my job. I can't take him in — in fact, I may have to give up my own flat. What I can do is spend a lot more time with him.'

'Sorry about your job — it's a bad time to be looking for work. But human company is exactly what he's needing. If you have time to work with him, you might reclaim his interest, turn him round again.'

Becky stared at the neat desk, blurring through sudden tears.

'The person who could turn him round was buried three years ago,' she said bleakly. 'I'll do what I can. Thank you.' She rose to go.

The nurse gently put a hand on her arm. 'Miss Calderwood, so far as I can see, the only problem your uncle has is that he feels completely useless. He is neither sick, nor senile. Stubborn, yes — but what man isn't? To turn him round, you simply need to convince him that you're needing him. Even critically ill people will always rally to a cry for help, respond to a feeling that they're being useful again. And Mr Medwin's far from ill . . .'

'Thank you,' Becky replied.

She steadied herself and walked firmly along the corridor, climbing the stairs to Noel's floor. Outside his door, she hesitated. Knocked. Silence.

Becky opened the door and stepped inside.

Noel was sitting beside the window, his chair angled to let him see out to the garden below. His head was drooping, chin almost resting on his chest. As if he'd fallen asleep, he made no move to see who had come into his room.

'Noel,' she said gently. 'It's me. Becky.'

No response. From outside came the muffled noises of distant voices, people walking, furniture scraping, trolleys moving, all the muted hubbub that makes up the sound-track of any hospital.

Becky hesitated, then picked up the second chair and carried it over to the window, setting it down opposite him. He still seemed asleep, even when she sat down in it and edged forward towards him.

She took one of his thin hands into her own. His skin was cold.

'Ella would be so angry,' she said quietly. 'She'd never have believed that you would simply turn your face to the wall, and give up on all of us.'

An eternity, before his head lifted slowly, moved round.

Faded blue eyes found hers, locked on.

'The world goes on, Noel,' she said. 'I know you're hurting. But I need you now . . . I need you more than at any other time in my life. Be there for me.'

The blue eyes were suddenly steady.

'Help me, Noel,' she said blindly. 'I've lost my job, in the teaching cuts . . . and without that job, how will I find the mortgage money? Everybody's cutting back, private sector and public sector alike. Where can I find another job? There *is* no work out there, not for anyone, let alone a single mother, with a child who's being bullied at his school. I'm almost out of my mind, with worry. I need someone strong to lean on, Noel. You've always been there, showing me how to land on my feet, how to move on with my life. I need you desperately, Noel, don't abandon me . . . '

It started as a shamefaced, manipulative trick to catch his attention. But somewhere along the line, she had become a little girl again, with a skinned knee from trying to jump much further than she was able. Turning blindly to her tough, worldly-wise substitute father, the steadfast anchor in her life. And it had all come tumbling out, words and tears together.

Becky felt his other hand cover hers. She looked up.

'Dinna fret,' he said, his voice dry from lack of use. He coughed. 'Can you keep a secret from that sister? She has eyes in the back of her head . . . '

'What secret?'

'My bedside cabinet. Bottom drawer. Under the pyjamas, right corner, at the back. It's only a quarter bottle, for emergencies. I'd say this is an emergency, wouldn't you? There's a packet of Polo mints, beside it — for confusion of the local Gestapo. Bring that out too. You have the glass, I'll drink from the bottle. Here, let me pour your dram . . . it's exactly what we're needing for a day like this.'

As he poured a small amount of whisky, Becky found herself smiling again, relief flooding through her. 'You crafty old devil,' she accused.

'Guilty, as charged.' He held out the glass. 'Let's trust the distiller to have put in the right amount of water. *Slainthe*!'

'They told me you had drifted into a world of your own.'

'And you, needing me?'

Becky sobbed, choked, the whisky burning her throat.

'Get it down you,' he said briskly. 'There's brighter minds than ours have turned to drink, to help them think.'

'The day is better already — now that you've decided to come back.'

'If a useless old uncle can't be a bad example to his favourite niece, what other use does he have?'

'I'm your only niece,' she protested.

'Doesn't change the logic. Right, let's cut through the flimflam to the subheads.' He stopped to take a sip of whisky, pulled a face. 'I'm out of practice,' he excused. 'This used to taste better. You've lost your job. You need time to find another one. And in the meantime, there's a mortgage to pay.'

'Is this where you pull a white rabbit out of your hat?' Becky asked hopefully.

'Never had a hat in my life. Or rabbits.' Thoughtfully, he screwed the cap back onto the whisky bottle, and reached for a mint to kill the smell. 'Can you hide this again?' he asked.

'How did you bring it here, in the first place?' she demanded.

'A good newspaperman never reveals his sources.' He grinned, the old devil-may-care glint in his eyes. 'OK, here's my first stab at a solution — with young Jonathon's problem uppermost in my mind. We need a change of scene for both of you. So, rent out your flat . . .'

'But . . .'

'Rent out your flat,' Noel said firmly. 'It will bring in enough money to pay your mortgage while you're looking for work. Next, find a new school for Jonathon, give him a fresh chance in life. And in doing that, follow your nose and look for work — any kind of work. Just as you would settle for any port in a storm.'

Becky's head reeled. 'But how?' she said. 'And where am I going to live?'

'Oh, didn't I say that? The *Ella Mae*, what else.'

The *Ella Mae* was his ancient narrowboat, converted from an even more ancient working barge. She had been the apple of Noel's eye. The magic carpet which had transported him and Ella all over Britain's canal network.

'But I don't know how to sail her!'

'I have someone in mind, to show you the ropes. Give you a crash course — not too literally, I hope — to make sure you can handle her anywhere. People set out in hired boats, after a ten-minute tutorial. So why not you, after a proper canal man has made sure you're safe.'

'But where do I put Jon in school?'

'Find a long-stay stretch on the canal — I know two or three places which are ideal. Then live in the *Ella Mae*, while you search

16

for work and get Jon into a school. Take whatever you can get, for both of you. Anything. It's only a short-term solution. Meanwhile, keep applying for proper teaching jobs, anywhere from Land's End to John o' Groats. Simple.'

Becky found herself swept along by his calm reasoning.

'Would it work?' she asked breathlessly.

'Why not? People live full-time in canal boats. Snug as the proverbial bug, with the stove lit and the curtains drawn in winter — although, God willing, you will have found a new teaching job and settled into your new home, by then.'

A sudden surge of optimism coursed through Becky.

'It would let me keep the flat,' she said.

'Exactly.'

'And give me time to find another job — a proper one.'

'Absolutely.'

'Noel,' she said. 'You are a genius.'

'Just a daft old man, with a head of teak . . . ' and he patted the white bandages round his brow.

'Not to mention a quart-bottle of whisky, hidden away.'

'So, nobody's perfect. Rules are made to be broken.'

'It might work,' Becky said slowly. 'I could make it work.'

'Never doubted you, not for a second.'

'Noel,' she said. 'Can I hug you?'

'Only if I can hug you back.'

Becky stretched across to the man who had always been such a strong and central figure in her life. Coming back from the dead, almost, to help her out again. Then a crazy but important idea flicked into her mind.

'On one condition,' she said. Too scared to think it through.

'Which is?' The faded blue eyes were steady.

'Come with us. Don't go back to your house, to rot. Show us what to do.'

'Me? I'd only get into your way.'

'Not you,' she said. 'There's cabin space for three, isn't there?'

'If I change my work den back into a cabin, for Jon.'

Becky took her courage in both hands. 'Please come,' she said. 'Because what would happen, if I left you here? They'd never let you go home. Then you really would drift off into that other world and they'd send you off long term into a nursing home. And your own house would be eaten up in a couple of years by their charges for a private room.'

'Was that what the dragon was telling you?'

'She's not a dragon.'

'She does a good imitation of one.'

'Deal or no deal?' Becky demanded.

Noel turned his face away, looking round his convalescent room, as if seeing it for the first time. She watched him slowly shake his head. 'Are you absolutely sure?' he asked her quietly. 'Absolutely, utterly sure that you want to saddle yourself with a daft old uncle who is nearly 200 years old . . . '

' . . . and smuggles whisky into convalescent homes. Yes, I'm sure.'

The steady eyes held hers for what seemed an eternity. While she had a moment of panic, wondering what she was letting herself in for. She saw him read her panic and wait quietly, patiently, for her to change her mind.

She would die first.

'I'm absolutely, utterly sure,' she repeated.

He held out his hand. 'Deal,' he said. He smiled with wry humour. 'This is a massive gamble for both of us, my lassie.'

'It beats waiting here, to take what life will throw at us,' she said.

He nodded again. 'I never was one for waiting,' he replied. 'And there's a place in my mind up north, in God's own country, that would give us all a fresh start. Let me take you there . . . '

Mike Preston rearranged his six-foot body across the floor of the steering well, struggling to find an extra half-inch for the arm which reached deep into the dark cubbyhole where the ancient diesel engine sulked. Waiting for some TLC. The electric engines in modern narrowboats were far less trouble, but Mike had a lifelong love of these old contrary originals.

He closed his eyes, working on finger-feel alone. There: his fingers closed on the fuel feed. Frowning, he tried to work it free. Oily fingers skidded on the oily pipe. Mike twisted his body a little more to force his shoulder still further under the floorboards, and tried again.

The phone rang in his office, relayed out to the boat-yard. He paused: would the caller go away? No. Each time the answerphone cut in, the ringing stopped — only to start up again, when the number was redialled. Someone was determined to reach him, in person.

Mike sighed. Like many big men, he was a gentle giant. Mostly. So long as nobody pushed him too hard. He uncoiled from the floor, reaching for an oily rag on which to wipe his hands.

In the early-morning sunlight, heavy dew

sparkled on the tufts of grass along the canal towpath. He walked, with barely any trace of his limp, across the yard and into his office, picking up the phone and glancing at the identification panel.

'Mr Medwin,' he said. 'Sorry, I was upside down in a boat. What can I do for you?' He listened, frowning. 'Not a problem. The *Ella Mae* is moored down at the end of the yard. I tied a tarpaulin over her in October, just like you asked. A couple of hours' work would take that off and drain her bilges . . . '

His knee hurt. Mike sat on the corner of the scarred desk, which had served three generations of owners. 'Sorry. Say again.'

The instructions were repeated. 'Yes . . . I can fuel her up with diesel, and take on fresh water. And check that the engine is working, likewise sterilize all the water systems. You'd be better getting a full service, leaving her ready to run. What? Convert the desk back into the original bunk? Should be easy. Want me to provision her, or . . . '

He massaged the knee, a gesture repeated fifty, maybe even a hundred times a day. Mike never counted, because he was generally unaware that he was doing it. A reflex action — closing the barn door after the horse had bolted.

He straightened. 'Take her down to

Ormskirk for you? Possibly, Mr Medwin, but let me check the office diary . . . ' Blackened fingers flicked over the oily corners of the pages. There were a couple of scribbled entries, but nothing he couldn't call up and postpone. It was too early in the season to be busy.

'Yes,' he finally replied. 'I can shuffle things around. If I work on the *Ella Mae* this afternoon, and get in some provisions, I can sail her down to Wigan by Thursday night. Then a day to go down the Flight — the lock-keepers will be on hand to help me, I won't have to do it all on my own. They're a decent bunch of lads. I can have her waiting for you at Ormskirk by Saturday morning. If I pull out all the stops, that's the quickest I can reach you.'

Frowning, he listened again. Whatever was being said at the other end, it clearly wasn't what Mike wanted to hear. Twice he tried to interrupt; each time, the voice at the other end of the phone talked over him.

Mike shook his head. 'Sorry, no way! I can't spare you a whole week of my time, Mr Medwin,' he finally said. 'If it was a hire boat, the yard would give your crew fifteen minutes' instruction, at best. Tell you what, I'll take your crew up through the Wigan Flight on Saturday — show them the ropes. By then, they'll know how to steer, moor, handle swing bridges, and locks. But, come Saturday night, I'm heading home. Leaving Sunday to catch up on what's happened here, in the yard.'

He listened, nodding, to the reply. 'OK,' he said. 'I'll meet you at 8 a.m. sharp.' He hesitated. 'How have you been keeping?' he asked, thinking that the old guy had looked pretty dodgy in the autumn. The pithy reply left him snorting with laughter. 'Great! Right, see you soon,' he said.

Absently, Mike put down the phone. Noel Medwin was a customer who went back through his dad's generation, maybe even back to his granddad. He and his dead wife, Ella, had always used the yard to service their boat between trips which wandered all over Britain. Then the wife had died, and the old boat had been claimed by cobwebs. Shame.

He was glad to hear that Noel and his boat were taking to the water again — but what did he mean by 'tunnelling out to escape'? Escape what? And who exactly were this crew he had to train? Was the old guy kosher, his marbles still lined up neatly, or was he going to sail down through Wigan to find the police and the social services waiting for him on the bank?

The man he remembered wouldn't go gaga in six months. Would he?

23

Mike grinned. For sure, things always happened when Noel Medwin was around — nothing had changed. The trip would be a busman's holiday, taking the *Ella Mae* down through Wigan's locks. That should work up a fair sweat . . .

A fair sweat, like in the old days. Sometimes he missed them, the limelight, the constant demands for interviews. Mostly he didn't, because he was back to doing the thing he loved — which was to work on boats.

He walked back across the yard, whistling. A sudden gust of spring breeze whisked a plastic bag towards him. Instinctively, his foot snapped out and brought it down. Before he could stop himself, he had switched feet and was kicking it.

He yelped. Bent down to massage that stupid knee again, then straightened, smiling wryly. Those days were gone. As in forever.

★ ★ ★

Kathy sighed: she was a lot less confident than she had sounded. The pep talk had been aimed as much at herself as Becky. Uneasily, she flipped through the Situations Vacant pages. There simply were no jobs in teaching locally — not even within long-haul commuting distance.

She drummed her fingers uneasily on the table. Step 1 had been to check and see what was on offer. Very little, it seemed. Step 2, she hadn't yet decided — but it would have to include some kind of physical involvement, because she wasn't engineered to sit down and wait.

She rose and moved with catlike fluidity over to the window, looking unseeingly down the street outside. If the mountain wouldn't come to Mohammed, then Mohammed must go to the mountain. Step 2, she decided, would be to update her CV, promoting herself as a blend of Wonderwoman and the Brain of Britain. That's what you had to do these days, market yourself as a brand, rather than simply tell the truth. Next she would print out about a dozen copies, with a covering letter saying: 'This is me, have you a job anywhere that needs to be done?' Then she would hand-deliver the letters, to every school in the district. Marketing herself.

She grinned. No bike, but Norman Tebbitt would be proud of her.

One thought led to another. Making a start on Step 2 would fill this afternoon but, right now, she needed to be out and running, feeling the blustery wind from the Ribble Estuary on her face. She could cut down to the promenade. At this time of the year, it would be shorn of its tourists. So she could plug in her iPod and run along the coast until her legs told her that it was time to turn and head for home.

That would get rid of doubts and frustrations, and maybe spark inspiration for her CV flights of fancy. It beat worrying.

Within five minutes, she was standing on her doorstep, a slender figure in tracksuit and well-scuffed trainers. She reached up, adjusting the iPod earpieces, then switched on. Already in her own world, she ran lithely down the street, heading for the seafront with the light-footed stride of a natural runner.

Behind her, the blustery wind sent dead leaves whirling and dancing in brown spirals, across the empty pavements.

* * *

Becky stared through her flat's front windows. It was too early in the year to become a nomad, but she was now committed to that course. Restlessly she turned, tidying cushions which she'd straightened only minutes before.

So far, it had been much easier than expected. The head teacher hadn't created a fuss — indeed had admitted that taking Jon away from her school might be the best way of solving the bullying problem. She had warned Becky that the education authorities would soon intervene, if Jon wasn't quickly placed in a new school, but had been happy to organize a list of work to be covered, so that Becky could teach him herself, until that new school was found.

The estate agents had been reassuring. She had a good choice — to rent, or sell. It was a nice flat, in a good location, and retiring couples were always looking for suburban ground-floor flats in Southport. Oddly enough, they had backed up Noel: why sell when the housing market was barely starting to recover? Better simply to rent, and pick your tenants carefully. Which they would do.

The front door opened. It was Jonathon, back from school. He pushed through into the lounge, hair ruffled by the wind, cheeks glowing.

'Well,' Becky said. 'Had a good day at school?'

'Sort of. Managed to stay invisible. Wasn't made the teacher's pet.'

Her son was bright, with the kind of instant understanding which hard-pressed teachers were too quick to applaud, making him more of a target than he already was. But 'invisible' was probably a code word for no bullying. After her last complaint, that had subsided

— the boys in question aware that they were being watched, and waiting for this new interest in them to die away.

She could tell him now, when all the i's were dotted. 'How would you feel about leaving that school forever?'

He looked at her puzzled, instantly aware that this was not a game.

She had planned to keep this low key, but it all came out in a rush. 'How would you like to live in a canal boat, while we look for a new job for me and a new home for us to stay in?'

Becky staggered as he hurled himself into her arms. 'I take it, that means a yes,' she said, her eyes filling. She felt him nod.

'When do we leave?' he asked, his face pressed deep into her.

'Is this weekend soon enough?'

He looked up at her, eyes shining. 'What's the boat like?' he asked. 'Is it painted and things? Does it have potted flowers on it . . . ?'

Becky laughed. 'I've never been aboard her, since I was about your age . . . '

But without waiting for her answer, he was dancing round the room. 'We're getting away from school!' he chanted.

'No you're not,' she said sternly. 'I'll be teaching you, until . . . '

Jonathon raced out of the room. 'I'm off to

28

pack!' he called over his shoulder.

Becky smiled wryly. That meant she'd probably have to unpack, then make sure that he was taking all the boring things — like clothes and schoolbooks. But some of his excitement lingered in the room. She felt herself respond.

A new beginning. Forced on her by circumstances, but giving her a chance to find a new life for both of them. With fresh scope for growth. For a few moments, the challenge left her exhilarated. Then her doubts returned, like crows to their rookery in the dusk.

So early in the year, to live like gypsies. Would the narrowboat be cold, and damp? Where was she going to find another job? She absolutely must. She was responsible, not just for herself but for her son. Worse, she was taking responsibility for an old man who was struggling to cope with life. Could she bring back to life the Noel Medwin she knew — or was she only causing further problems, maybe hastening his decline? Was she mad?

From across the hall, she heard her small son singing. A noise which seemed strange, because she hadn't heard him sing for years. There had been no reason for him to sing.

Until now.

Becky's shoulders straightened. She couldn't, she wouldn't, let him down.

2

The taxi drew up with a squeal of brakes that echoed across the early-morning stillness of the canal basin. Closed and boarded grey buildings huddled together, above a cluster of moored narrowboats.

'That's us,' said Noel. 'There's the *Ella Mae* — down at the canal side.'

'It's got smoke, coming out of its chimney,' Jonathon said excitedly.

'Why not? There's an iron stove inside,' Noel replied. 'Mike will have the kettle on, waiting for us.' He tugged the thick woollen jacket more tightly round himself, shivering.

'Leave your case here,' Becky urged. 'I'll come back for it.'

'The crew pulls its weight — or it's not a crew at all,' Noel said firmly. He lifted his small case. 'You too, Jon. A sailor carries his own kitbag . . . but don't try to sling that case over your shoulder. Good lad. That leaves your mum with two to carry. She comes cheaper than native porters . . . '

Becky smiled. She should have been worried, scared; instead she was full of excitement and fresh optimism — Noel's quiet and careful work. She sniffed the sharp air. The morning had the feel of a new start in life, she thought. High trees, standing silent and shrouded in mist; heavy dew glistening on the fields beyond the marina and on the tarpaulins of the moored boats. Only the distant sound of traffic, already muted as if it belonged to another world. No movement anywhere, not even a single rook across the sky.

As if the world was waiting for them to write a new beginning.

The cabin door opened on the *Ella Mae*. She watched a tall figure climb up the steps from the cabin and close the door behind him to keep in the warmth. It was a morning for rubbing your hands together — only hers were full of suitcases, and even the minimal packing that Noel had insisted on was heavy.

She saw the man hesitate, then step from the steering well onto the bank and walk easily towards them. Broad-shouldered, untidy dark hair which needed cut, quiet grey eyes in a face burned dark from exposure to the wind.

'You're right on schedule, Mr Medwin,' he said.

'It was Noel to your dad, and your granddad before him,' Noel said mildly.

They shook hands. The suitcase was

gathered easily into a large paw, then the canal man reached for one of Becky's cases. She found herself looking up into calm and steady eyes. 'I'm Mike,' he said easily. 'Mike Preston.'

'Rebecca,' she replied. 'Most people call me Becky.'

'I've got the kettle boiling,' said Mike. 'Why don't we all go down and have a mug of tea while you're stowing your luggage.' Silently, he thought: Well done, Noel, they haven't come laden down with clothes that can't be stored. A good start to their new life. One that showed this Becky to be willing to listen and learn. She'd have to do a lot of that, to cope with living full-time on a canal boat. Would she be too posh and sheltered to adjust?

He liked his first impressions. Not a head-turner, just slim and competent and nice. Too many lines of worry around her eyes and mouth. Noel would sort these out — as would the sheer joy of living in the open air and travelling.

'Watch your feet on the gunwale, as you step aboard,' he said. 'I'll go first . . . pass over your cases. Steady yourself as you step aboard — one hand for yourself and the other for the ship, that's what old sailors used to say. It still applies, even to canal boats.'

The cabin was just as Becky remembered. Warm and snug, neat blue curtains drawn back to show crisp white lace curtains underneath. Beneath these, two sets of comfortable cushioned bench seats on either side of the table, with a blackened iron stove taking up a corner on the other side. Between the cabin door and this, storage cupboards, with a row of hooks for mugs or brass and iron cooking utensils. The neat kitchen was tucked onto the same side as the table. With four of them standing there, it was full but not crowded.

'Main cabin's up in the bows,' said Mike. 'I take it that's yours, Noel?' But it was to Becky that he looked; she nodded. 'Fine. The small cabin lies port side — that's to the left as you look — of the passageway. I rebuilt the bed, Noel, under the window where your desk was . . . '

He neatly sidestepped, and grinned, as Jonathon hurtled past.

It was a nice grin, Becky thought. The man was taking real pleasure in her small son's excitement and need to explore his new home.

'Your cabin, Becky, is this lounge space, once it converts at night. The tabletop drops down between the seat boxes, to make up a bed base. Rearrange the cushions, to make your mattress. Your bedding is stowed under the seats — see, here's the cupboard door.' He lifted the crisp tablecloth aside.

'Mum! Come and see!' Jonnie was beside himself with excitement.

Mike waved her past. 'It's better once everybody's sitting down. More space. They don't call them narrow-boats for nothing. They were designed so that two of them can sit side by side in any of the canal locks. Saves water — and that's the most important thing in any canal. No water, no passage . . . '

Becky eased through. Then her hand was grabbed and she was hauled into the small second bedroom in the boat. A single bunk, neatly made with a fresh-looking duvet cover. Clean curtains. But what her son was pointing at was a poster hanging from the wall — two posters, she realized, as she turned to look. Instantly transforming the working den she remembered into a boy's room.

On one wall hung a huge blue and white team photograph of Wigan FC, the signatures of all the players scrawled across their images. And on the facing wall, an action poster in red of one of the best-known faces in British football.

'I coach kids,' Mike said quietly. 'I got the Wigan boys to sign the poster for another lad

— but he dropped out of the coaching sessions and it's been cluttering up my office. The Stevie Gerrard poster I've had for years, waiting for the right lad to turn up. Its wait is over.'

'Thank you,' she said, her throat constricting.

'Not a problem,' Mike said. 'I'm off to make the tea . . . '

He headed into the cabin, to find Noel sitting at the table, looking around him, a sad and nostalgic smile on his face. Too many shadows present.

'You've had everything washed and cleaned,' Noel commented.

'It was damp and dingy from over-wintering. There's a laundry and ironing service in the village. I got them to run everything through. First impressions count — especially to a woman.' Mike nodded silently back to where Becky was still in her son's bedroom. They could hear the boy's excited voice.

'Thanks,' said Noel. 'It was vital that we started off on the right foot, keeping her thinking positively — and you've done that. I can't thank you enough . . . '

'Who takes milk, and who takes sugar?' Mike asked, turning away.

★   ★   ★

Kathy ran along the sandy promenade, heading back from Martin Mere and into the wind from the sea. She had her earpiece in and was singing along to the track which was playing.

Her letters had been delivered. Now she could only wait — and run. She had a feeling that the treads on her trainers would grow smooth before she had a reply, but that first step must always be taken before you start on any long march — ask Chairman Mao.

She loved feeling fit, the wind blowing through her hair. On days like this, she felt as if she could run a marathon, without stopping for a break.

Ahead of her, she spotted another runner. A man.

Gradually, she overtook him. 'Hiya,' she said.

'Hi,' he answered.

For a few paces, they ran together.

'Great wind for running,' he said. 'Keeps you nice and cool.'

She glanced across. Mid-thirties, she guessed, but some speckles of grey in the hair at his temples. Weather-beaten brown — another regular runner. Kathy slowed to his pace. It was always good to have company for a bit, with someone who was like-minded.

'Been out to the Mere,' she said. 'Yourself?'

'No. Cut in across the fields back there. I've work waiting for me, couldn't manage the full route today.'

She nearly told him that she was out of work. Boring — unless you were unemployed yourself. 'I usually run at night,' she said.

'I'm busy then.'

She waited for a few strides, but he didn't elaborate. 'OK,' she said. 'I'll be doing some morning running — maybe see you again . . .'

There was an imp in Kathy. Road runners often share a distance, side by side; then one of them accelerates away. Kathy took a perverse pleasure in running with men, then leaving them floundering in her wake. She lengthened her stride.

He casually matched her increase in speed.

She grinned, then quietly poured on more pace.

He matched her again and, from the corner of her eye, she could see that he was smiling slightly. OK, so he was fit. This was a real challenge, but she would burn him off.

She didn't. They became two athletes, no longer talking, just settling to the task of pushing the other to breaking point. Only neither broke.

As they came into the town's front, she panted: 'I cut up here.'

'I'm a bit further on . . . take care.'

To her annoyance, his breathing seemed easier than her own.

She paused. 'You can run,' she said wryly. 'I usually leave them floundering with sustained pace like that.'

'Once I could run,' he said. 'Now, I play at it.'

'Bye.'

'Bye . . . ' He watched her fleet-footed figure turn up into the town, then set off again himself. At a slower pace. Now she was gone, he started panting too . . . no further need for mind games. He grinned. With luck, their training runs would converge again. Triggering another battle of their wills.

He looked forward to that. He liked her style.

*   *   *

Mike's eye caught Becky's. 'Look,' he said apologetically. 'If we're going to go up the Wigan Flight today, we need to get underway. The locks close by dusk.'

Becky glanced at the table, now a comfortable clutter of mugs and plates.

'I'll wash up,' said Noel. 'Jon can dry. You'll need your feet clear upstairs anyway, not being crowded by spectators.'

Becky's shoulders squared: this was the real

start to her new life.

'Right,' she said, her heart skipping a beat.

'Relax,' Mike said easily. 'Everything moves slowly on a canal, so you can take your time. The more you hurry, the more likely you are to get it wrong.' He led the way up the steps through the folding cabin doors, out into the cold.

'What do I do first?' Becky asked determinedly.

'Start the engine. See this lever down here — that's the throttle. You can reach down and move it with your hand. But it's set at a height where you can nudge it forward or back, by your knee, leaving your hands free. Nudge it to neutral, before you start up.' He pushed the lever to its original position. 'Now you do it,' he instructed. 'Move it back until you feel it clunk.'

Becky swallowed, but the cold metal lever slipped easily back into neutral.

'What's next?' she asked.

'Press that button. Like this . . . '

His large hand gently took, then pushed firmly through, her index finger to the starter. The engine coughed, then growled beneath her feet. He took her hand away, then let go.

Her skin tingled, where his fingers had gently held her.

'Well done,' he said. 'Now the dodgy bit.

I'll take the tiller, you step onto the bank and release the ropes. Coil the bow rope on the cabin top — you'll need it later. Then release the stern rope. Gently put your foot against the boat and ease her bows out. Not too far, because you have to step back on board. No jumping — that's when accidents happen.'

Becky stepped onto the canal bank, walked forward to the front rope. She hesitated, then saw that it had been left simply to pull the end of the rope, and the knot would be released. Easy work, the rope damp and cold in her hands. She half-coiled it, and leaned forward to drop it onto the cabin roof.

The engine's beat rose a little, as she walked back to the stern and released the second knot.

'Just a gentle push . . . that's it, with the sole of your foot.'

Becky leaned, unsure, against the boat's gunwale. Felt it move slightly.

'Enough. Now, step back on board.' The same calm instruction.

And she was back in the steering well, safe and sound.

'See,' Mike said. 'Our bows are easing out from the bank . . . all we have to do is nudge the lever forward, get the engine working . . . that's us underway.'

The *Ella Mae* settled to a steady

putt-putt-putt, and the bank began to slide slowly past. 'Keep to the right,' said Mike. 'Water has different rules from roads. Let me settle her down, then you can take the tiller.'

'Me? I don't know how to steer!'

'So, you have ten hours, to learn. I'll help at first . . . that's it, stand here beside the throttle lever.'

Her heart racing, Becky took over the high brass tiller. It was icy cold to the touch. Then she felt a warm hand slip over her own.

'If you want to steer to the right,' said Mike, 'ease the tiller the opposite direction . . . but not too much. Like this. And if you want to go to the left, swing it to the right. Always in the opposite direction. We've got the canal to ourselves, let's go out into the middle and you take over.'

Becky gulped, clinging onto the tiller like grim death.

'Don't dent it!' he grinned. 'Ease off. Just watch the prow — that's the pointy bit at the front. Let me see you steer a little right . . . no, be patient, you have forty tonnes of boat moving, she takes time to answer, and if you steer too far then you've got to correct. A little at a time, unless in emergencies. No hurry, everything's slow motion at 3 mph. That's it.'

'These ducks!' panicked Becky. 'I'm going to hit them!'

'Don't be daft,' he smiled. 'They can swim twice as fast as you. Hold your course. They'll get out of your way.'

Which they did, with room to spare.

With the canal to themselves, the sun still rising over the trees, Becky was starting to enjoy the feel of the old canal boat moving through the water. The bows drifted a little to the right — and she found herself instinctively steering against it. She watched them straighten, then drift to the left. Her correction this time was exact — and instinctive.

'You're a fast learner,' Mike complimented. 'Not many women are.'

'I beg your pardon!' Becky exclaimed.

He waved a placating hand. 'Technical stuff. Men usually pick it up quicker — it's like reading maps.'

'I can read a map,' she snapped.

He grinned. 'OK, I take your word for it, Cap'n.'

She blinked. 'What?'

'Captain. There is one ruler on any boat, and that's the captain. On board, he — or she — is God. Their word undisputed. Theoretically, you can keelhaul your crew for indiscipline. But I doubt there's enough water to do that right now . . . '

That was better, he thought: he had her

laughing. He pointed ahead. 'Here's our first obstacle. A swing bridge.'

Becky peered over the cabin roof. 'Do we squeeze under it?'

'No room. We have to stop, and open it.'

'How do we stop?' She glanced down.

Mike laughed outright. 'There's no brake pedal. Lower the revs and she'll slow down. Go on. That's it, nudge the lever back a little . . . a bit more. Let her slow down, and coast in towards the bank. Good. Now nudge the lever back, beyond neutral. That's reverse, and the propeller's stopping our forward movement. Back into neutral. Give me the tiller. Take the stern rope and when she touches, step ashore — no jumping.'

Becky found herself on dry land, threading the rope through a rusting metal hoop on the bank.

'A couple of turns,' she heard. 'Then finish it the way you got it before, if you can remember how.'

She straightened, to find him smiling beside her, a steel L-shaped crank in his hand. 'Let's go,' he said. 'I'll show you how to turn a bridge round on its axis . . . '

As they waited for road traffic to ease, he grinned. 'Get used to being hated, by every motorist you hold up. Right, press this button, that activates the signals and stops the traffic. Fit the handle on like this . . . and turn like mad. It's low-gearing, not heavy. Here, you do it.'

She found herself turning the handle, hair falling over her face.

'Good old Noel,' she heard him say. 'He's got the tiller. He's going to take her through himself. Your boy's unloosing the rope.'

'If he falls in . . . '

'He won't. This is *Boy's Own* adventure stuff. Look at him, it's like Noel has given him a birthday present!'

Becky blinked back tears. This wasn't her frightened son, any more. Just an ordinary boy, taking orders from a man — and enjoying it. She watched him step nimbly on board, and hold onto the cabin roof as Noel brought their new home putt-putting through beneath them.

'Now close the bridge,' Mike said. 'You do it. You need to know.'

Becky spun the handle, marvelling at how a whole section of road could pivot so easily on ancient engineering. She felt it clunk gently and the mechanism lock.

'Press the button,' Mike said. 'Set the lights to green. Always give the motorists a friendly wave — like this. Make them feel bad for all the nasty things they've been muttering.'

But the motorists were smiling and waving

too, as they sped past.

Mike had that effect on people, she thought wryly.

'Come on,' he said. 'Only eight more bridges, before we reach the Wigan locks — you'll be a world expert, by then. Between the three of you, all the jobs have been decided. You to open and close the bridge. Noel to steer her through and moor her for you. And your lad to act as cabin boy, hopping off and on. Well done, Cap'n. You run a tight ship.'

There was a twinkle in his eye, which became a grin. Becky felt herself smiling too. 'I could murder another mug of tea,' she panted.

'You're the captain. Order your crew to make one.'

★   ★   ★

'What are these big tin cans on our cabin roof?' asked Jonathon.

'Water cans,' replied Noel. 'In the old days, boats didn't have water tanks below. The entire canal family lived and slept in the one cabin, which was where we have the table and the kitchen. Beyond that, the rest of the boat was an empty hull, with tarpaulins draped over it. They carried whatever they could get, for a few shillings to someplace else, up and down the canal. So they kept their fresh water in these big old cans, up top. Old working boats like the *Ella Mae* still keep them on the roof — it's a tradition.'

'Why are they painted?'

Noel increased the revs slightly and steered carefully through beneath the swing bridge. 'Another tradition,' he said. 'Canal families used to be Romanies — gypsies from Europe. They loved bright colours. And that's why so many canal boats have castles painted on them, the folk-memories the Romanies brought with them. Some boats have flowers painted. The canal system runs through the Potteries, where the fashion was to paint roses on the china. The Romanies copied these flower patterns from their china cargoes onto their boats. It gave them something cheerful to look at in the winter, when the land beside the canal was dead.' He eased off the revs and glided gently to the bank. 'Step, don't jump — and don't forget the rope, like last time.'

'Aye, aye, sir,' said Jonathon. Thinking that this sailor's term should really be 'No, no,' in the circumstances.

'Would you listen to them?' Becky panted, working to close her fifth swing bridge behind them. 'Noel's adopting him — just like he once adopted me . . . '

46

Kathy wasn't one for hanging about. Within minutes of getting the idea at the supermarket tills, she was speaking to a supervisor. Within minutes of that, she was being ushered into the manager's office, still carrying her shopping.

The manager listened, nodding, to the supervisor's whispered explanation, his eyes set on Kathy. 'So,' he finally said. 'You want a job?'

'Yes, please.'

'And you've worked the tills before?'

'When I was a student — it helped to put me through the university, then teacher training.'

'Which brands?'

Kathy blinked: he would mean which supermarket chains, she guessed. She told him, trying to remember how long she had worked for each of them

He grimaced. 'You're a bit overqualified for this. Some of the guys might give you a hard time because of that . . . '

'I can hold my own.'

The grimace became a smile. 'Dare say you can. OK. We've no full-time work right now, but you need to prove to us on a part-time basis that you can hack it. I can give you three

47

days a week — probably in half-shifts. You'll have to fit into the gaps we have in our staffing, and these might not always suit you. And you'll be expected to help out with the shelf-stacking, when there's no call for you on the tills.'

'Not a problem.'

The manager rose, shook her hand. 'Jean here will take you through the paperwork. Best of luck. Any serious problems, bring them to her — or me. Minor problems, you're expected to sort these out yourself.'

'I understand.' He meant cat-spats. Kathy gathered her bags again.

Half an hour later, she was walking home, a broad smile on her face. Her first week's work already organized, and her first overtime looming. She had no illusions: the work oscillated between boring and being run off your feet. But anything was better than hanging about, waiting for the phone to ring and the post to come. When neither ever did.

She was whistling when she reached her flat. Going into her kitchen, she dumped her bags on the worktop and filled the kettle. A coffee would go down very nicely. Pity she'd nobody to share her good news with . . .

Only, she had. Did mobile phones work on canal boats? So far as she knew, they worked anywhere. One way to find out. She opened her phone, went to contacts and scrolled down to Becky's number.

What was her friend doing, she wondered, listening. Had she fallen into the canal yet? Or got seasick?

'Rebecca Calderwood . . . '

'Well, Becky. Have you met the Ancient Mariner yet?' Kathy demanded.

'He's standing right beside me — aren't you, Noel?' Kathy heard a gurgle of laughter, then: 'You're not old enough to understand what he's just replied . . . '

★ ★ ★

'One last shove,' urged Mike, as the light faded. He was leaning at her side, his back against the lock gate's ancient wooden beam, helping her to close it now that the *Ella Mae* was through.

Becky felt like she had run a marathon. It had taken them all afternoon to rise through the 22 locks of the Wigan Flight. The first few locks were a total mystery as Mike and the lock keepers told her what to do. Now, she could go through lock gates in her sleep.

She felt the beam bump slowly against her back: the gates were closed.

'I know,' she said wearily. 'Now we wind the paddles down, to make the gates more

49

watertight. I'll do it. The crank's here, at my feet.'

He watched her stubbornly winding down the ancient mechanism. Halfway up the Flight he had seen her study blistered palms. You get callouses the hard way in canal travel. His own hands were tough as leather and rough as sandpaper.

She would do, he thought. This was a woman with grit and determination.

'Back to your ship,' he said gently. 'We'll moor her a couple of hundred yards up the bank. There's a decent canal-side pub up there. You can buy a meal — and save yourself the cooking.'

Becky looked at him gratefully. He had coaxed her through the longest and hardest-working day in her life, never once raising his voice, or sounding impatient, always making sure she could handle everything she would have to face alone, when he was gone. But quietly doing his share, helping out.

'Won't you stay for a meal?' she asked. 'We couldn't have managed this without you.'

'No, I'll have to go,' he replied. 'I'll walk down to the bus route, and catch a bus to Burnley. Get another to Foulridge from there — or phone a mate to collect me. I'll see you safely moored. Noel's had as much as he can cope with, today — more than he's done in months, I suspect.'

'He's more like the Noel of old,' she marvelled. 'Not the old man who drew back into his shell when he lost my aunt.'

'She was one feisty lady,' Mike smiled.

'She was everything to him — they had no children.'

'But now you and Jonathon have given him a new purpose in life.'

'I hope so.'

Evening was falling on the canal. Already lights were springing up in the dusk below them. They had climbed through Wigan and were now looking down on the sprawling town. Up ahead, she could see two other canal boats moored, lights already lit in the cabin windows. Beyond them, lights were showing at the canal-side pub. They had passed dozens of these on their way here, once watering holes for the boatmen who lived and worked on the canal, now cheerful village pubs or characterful inns in the heart of the docklands.

'I wish you could stay the night,' she said. 'Go home tomorrow.'

'No buses — and not enough room in the boat. It's OK, I'm less than a couple of hours from home. Road travel's a whole lot faster than struggling through swing bridges and locks.'

He held the stern rope while she stepped aboard, and she sensed a hand near her elbow, if she stumbled. Typical Mike: considerate, without making a fuss of it. She was going to miss his calm, strong presence. Today had been tough, so much to learn, the terrain the most difficult they would face, up to the Yorkshire Dales. Tomorrow, she would be totally on her own, with her crew.

Would they remember all their lessons from today?

They waved him off, once he had helped them moor the *Ella Mae*. A tall figure, travel bag lost in a huge hand, walking down the lane between the pub and the straggling houses. Then he was gone.

'You don't often get that,' Noel said quietly. 'Three real gentlemen — in every sense of the word — in three successive generations. You would never think that he was once the toughest striker in top-flight football. Hard, but fair. He got his share of English caps, before that knee injury. It happened before we sent our millionaire players over to specialist sports surgeons in America, and it finished his career. Such a shame. He was good.'

'Was he famous?' Jonathon asked.

'He's still a living legend to fans in Leeds and Newcastle.'

'You'd never guess,' said Becky. 'Right. Hands washed, then we crawl to the pub for supper.'

'Not me,' Noel said apologetically. 'I'm knackered. Take young Jon up, and get them to plate three meals for us. It's common, near the canal. They trust you to bring back the plates — already washed. I'll set the table.'

'Are you OK, Noel?' she asked quietly.

'Never been better. Go on. I'm hungry. Take Jon as your bodyguard.'

A gentle jest, but Becky saw her son's shoulders stiffen, and his head come up proudly. Ready to protect his mum.

'Noel,' she said. 'You are a magician.'

'Just a newspaperman. A chameleon. Changing into whatever shape I need to be. Invisible, always watching, always taking notes. Unless from my wallet.'

'This meal's on me,' she laughed.

The pub was quiet, the staff friendly, and the smell of food made her realize how hungry she was, and how long it had been since they had eaten. They hurried back to the boat, the foil-wrapped dishes warm in her hands.

On the bank, she stopped. Swallowed. Their new home: light shining cheerfully through its curtained windows, the cabin warm against the nip of cold which was coming down. And the table set, neat as any restaurant. With an opened bottle of wine already breathing.

'Are you going to make a habit of smuggling booze in your cases?' She pointed an accusing finger at Noel.

He grinned up at her. 'Only when it's needed,' he said.

She unwrapped the foil and set the plates down in front of them.

Noel carefully poured wine into their glasses. 'There's a Coke in the fridge for you,' he said to Jonathon. As the lad rose to get it, he raised his glass. 'To our future, Becky. May it give us not what we want, but what we need, to grow.'

They gently clinked glasses.

'Noel,' she said. 'You're a wise old bird. Are we really going to make it — cope with locks, bridges, jobs and schools and everything?'

'Why not?' he answered. 'The day-to-day stuff is not a problem — we'll be working through that as a team. It's the bigger picture which is important. Only you can build your future. Only you can choose where you really want to go . . . '

3

For the very first time since they had started out, three days before, there was real warmth in the sun. They basked, rather than huddled, in the steering well, as the *Ella Mae* slowly putt-putted along the canal. The flatlands of the Lancaster Pool dropped behind them, then the seven-lock stretch of Withnell Fold — child's play, after the Wigan Flight. They found themselves navigating eastwards through a steep and thickly wooded valley to Blackburn, the noise of the motorway drumming down through the trees.

'Why is there a path at the side of the canal?' asked Jonathon.

'An echo of the past,' said Noel. 'Diesel engines were only put into canal boats from the 1930s. Before then, they were towed by teams of horses with one of the canal family leading them. There were stables in all the villages, for the horses overnight — or the horses were simply tethered to feed off the grass at the side of the towpath.'

'Cool!' said Jonathon.

'Not if you were a horse,' smiled Becky. 'Pulling forty tonnes was sheer hard work.'

'At least forty tonnes,' corrected Noel. 'Some canal boats were up to twice as long as us, and sixty to eighty tonnes.'

'Did the *Ella Mae* have a team of horses?' Jonathon wondered.

'Probably one, maybe two horses.'

'Did they eat hay?'

'They were thin and hungry. They ate anything — grass, weeds, even leaves from the bushes as they walked past.'

'Cool!' Jonathon said.

'From the *Waterways Guide*, that was Millfield Bridge we just went under,' Becky muttered. 'We'll soon be in Blackburn. There's a half-dozen locks through the town and I think we should stop now for lunch.'

'There are some moorings up ahead,' said Noel. 'Let's have a break. And I think there's a nice place to moor, near a lake, just before we reach Norden. It's about as far as you can get from the M65 . . . so it should be more peaceful there.'

'I see it,' said Becky, studying the map. Bridges and locks meant even slower travel than before. She calculated, 'Then that will take us to supper time — you've done this route before, haven't you?'

'Often,' said Noel. 'Blackburn's about halfway along the length of the canal. It's only about forty miles further — four days' sailing

— to where I'm planning to take you.'

He studied her face: its worry lines were already fading, her skin browning from constant exposure to the wind. Another Romany in the making, he thought wryly. 'Well, lassie, how do you like living rough?'

'Brilliant!' said Becky.

'And you, Jon?' smiled Noel.

'It's cool,' said Jonathon.

'We're going to have to increase that vocabulary,' Noel sighed.

★ ★ ★

The wind across the Ribble Estuary made running a physical challenge. Kathy had her iPod on and was humming along with it. Then the mood changed, and one of her favourite tracks started playing. Her humming broke into song and she started giving the lyrics big licks.

Suddenly, her voice faltered, as she became conscious of someone running alongside her. 'Sorry,' she said, taking out the earpiece. 'Didn't know anyone was there . . . where have you come from? Been short-cutting across the fields again?'

The suntanned face broke into a grin. 'No. I've been overtaking you, from way back, and decided to slow down and share a mile or two.'

Kathy was outraged. People didn't overtake her — she did the overtaking. 'I must have got caught up in singing, and slowed down,' she muttered darkly.

'Then it must have been a very long song. You were only a tiny dot on the horizon, when I saw you first.'

'You're fibbing!'

'Cross my heart.'

'But you're not even panting,' she accused.

'These last two races we've had have got me back into shape.'

They shared a wry grin, knowing the other brought out the worst — or was it the best — in them. Three times they had tried to run each other into the ground, without succeeding. Two fit athletes, enjoying the contest.

'You weren't out running yesterday morning,' he said.

'I was working a half-shift at the supermarket.'

He looked surprised. 'I didn't know you worked at a supermarket,' he said.

'Only just started. I was a teacher. Now I'm out of work, looking for another teaching job.'

'That's tough,' he said. 'Not a good time to find a new job.'

'Meanwhile, working at the tills makes ends meet.'

'Absolutely.' He hesitated. 'My name's

David. David Harrison.'

'Kathy Woodford.'

'How long have you been teaching? Like the work?'

'Love it. I love watching a kid improve, and thinking: I did that . . . I made the difference . . . But if they're not willing, you can't teach them, so the first thing you have to do is get them to accept you. Treat them as equals, let them see you're human. Never talk down to them, or at them, treat them like another adult almost . . . ' She stopped. 'You're trying to get me out of breath before we start,' she accused. 'That's cheating.'

'Me? Do I look like somebody who would cheat?'

'You're a runner. You would make your granny climb three flights of stairs, before you raced her!'

David laughed. 'Absolutely. Otherwise, she'd beat me.'

'We're two of a kind. What do you do for work, yourself?'

'I'm an architect. Have my own small practice, working from home.'

'So you run when you need to take a break?'

'Just about.' A smile tugged at the corners of his mouth, and he gently increased his stride, moving away from her. 'Bye,' he said.

'See you tomorrow.'

'Good try.' Effortlessly, she came level. 'See you tomorrow,' she said, and accelerated.

He stayed with her, then, when she eased off, crammed on more pace.

For a second, she was stranded, then gradually fought herself back alongside him. 'That was sneaky,' she panted. 'Race you to the pier. Last one's a . . . '

She found herself talking to his back.

'Right!' she said indignantly. 'If that's the way you want it . . . '

Fifteen minutes later, they were hunched side-by-side, hands on knees and whooping for breath to feed oxygen into their aching, burning muscles.

'We're going to kill ourselves if we go on like this,' he finally gasped.

'I won,' she wheezed.

'In your dreams!'

They grinned at each other.

Kathy was a modern woman. When the idea came to her, she didn't waste time weighing it up. 'I'm off-shift tonight,' she panted. 'How about meeting for dinner? I'll fill you full of rice pudding, then race you again tomorrow.'

A shadow crossed his face.

'I can't,' he said. 'I don't do nights.'

Kathy's face burned. 'Not a problem,' she said brightly. 'Well, I'm off — there could be fifty letters waiting, all offering me a job. See you.'

She turned, and ran blindly through the tourist shops towards the Arcade, her stride and breathing ragged, her body not yet recovered. Running hurt. More than it should have done.

'Rats!' she thought. She'd blown it. Too much in-his-face. Pity. She liked the man, as in really liked, as in was interested in exploring what this strange, racing friendship could build into.

David watched her go, and shook his head.

'It's not like that,' he said quietly. 'Not like that at all . . . '

With heavy legs, and a heavier heart, he began to jog across the town.

⋆   ⋆   ⋆

They left the industrial landscapes behind, crossed the small aqueduct at Nelson, and climbed through the locks into countryside again at Barrowford. Another long day, with more than its share of locks — they were reaching the Pennines summit of the canal towards which they had climbed steadily since leaving Ormskirk.

'Where's Mike Preston's boatyard?' Becky asked casually.

Too casually, she thought, and frowned.

Noel didn't notice. 'At the Wharf, just beyond the Foulridge Tunnel,' he replied. 'On the edge of the village.'

'And he's definitely coming over to take us through?'

'Yes. Only experienced skippers are allowed to navigate the tunnel. It can be seriously tight, if you meet another canal boat coming in the opposite direction — no place for amateurs. Let's get to Wanless Bridge, before we phone him.'

Jonathon climbed into the steering well.

'Have you finished your homework?' Becky asked sternly.

'All done. When do we get to the tunnel? Tell me about it, Noel.'

'It's a mile long, right through the hill. Dug out with picks and shovels and human sweat and the odd blast of black powder, that's what people used before they had dynamite. It's the only stretch of the entire canal where there is no towpath. That would have meant too big a tunnel for engineering knowledge back then — and they'd never have got horses through it anyway. Only pit ponies would ever tolerate that amount of darkness.' He paused. 'Have you heard about the Foulridge cow, Becky?'

'No, but I sense I'm going to hear it now.'

'It's a true story.' Noel turned to Jonathon. 'When we come to the tunnel, it looks just like a hole in the hill, with a stone wall built around it. 'The Hole in the Wall' is what the locals call it. At the far side, one day in 1912, a cow lost its footing and rolled down the hill and into the canal. *Ker-splash!*'

'And?' said Jonathon.

'Some canal people tried to rescue it, while a villager ran to fetch the farmer. The cow didn't want to be rescued. She turned and swam into the tunnel, disappearing into the darkness. A canal family punted their boat into the tunnel after her, holding up a paraffin lamp to try and see where she was. They found her still swimming, and followed her right through to the end of the tunnel, 1,640 yards away. The poor cow was exhausted. But the farmer was waiting, and locals helped to rope her and pull her out.'

Noel grinned at Becky. 'Reports say that the cow was revived by vast amounts of ale — but how much of that reached the cow, and how much was consumed by the rescuers, we'll never know.'

'Did she live?' asked Jonathon.

'Until she was a very old lady. And she still holds the record for the fastest 1,640 yards ever swum by a cow . . . '

'Noel! You're making that up!' Becky accused.

'I'm not!' he replied indignantly. 'You can still see photos of the rescue in the local pub at Foulridge.'

'I'm phoning Mike,' sighed Becky. 'What's his number?'

★　★　★

David Harrison paused in the driving rain. No one ahead, he was sure of that. He peered back through the gloom towards the town end of the promenade. The road behind was equally empty — for the second day in succession.

Go on, or turn back?

Mentally, he flipped a coin . . . but was jogging forward, before his invisible coin hit the ground. The longer he stayed on the road, the better the chance he had of crossing paths again. And maybe, just maybe, finding a way of explaining to her — and himself — something which had tied him down for years.

Maybe her shifts had changed, and she couldn't run mornings?

Maybe she had changed her running route — as he often did himself, to prevent boredom.

There were a limited number of supermarkets in the town. Maybe, if he took the morning off and visited all of them? Did his weekly shopping, two items at a time? He shook his head.

She might have decided that enough was enough. No further contact.

If she had, then he must respect her decision. Such a pity. It was years since he'd felt attracted to another woman. So long, he had almost forgotten how to react. From the start, he'd sensed in her a woman who was unique, someone with whom he could build a stronger bond than simply running.

Head down, he plodded along the empty promenade.

The sea wind blew away the rain and shredded the clouds which had carried it. A weak and watery sun spilled through, then strengthened. It lit up the flat marshland all around him, bringing into it both colour and fresh life.

But it didn't even touch the edges of the dark cloud in his heart.

★   ★   ★

'Should we be wearing hard hats?' Becky asked nervously.

'Only if the water level rises.' Mike's eyes were twinkling.

'And will it?' Jonathon asked eagerly.

Mike shook his head. 'The canal's main supply is from the Foulridge reservoir, and the amount of water released is tightly controlled. We're safe.'

'How do we see in the dark?' asked Jonathon.

'Switch on our headlights — just like a car,' replied Noel.

'What if we see headlights coming at us from the other end?'

'We stay on the right and edge past each other.'

Mike turned to Becky. 'If you've waterproofs, put them on. There's usually a lot of water dripping from the tunnel roof. And if it's been raining a lot, it can be pretty mucky.'

He smiled. 'Permission to take control of your ship, Cap'n?'

Did anything ever cause this man to flap, Becky wondered. 'Permission granted,' she replied. 'But you pay for repairs to any dents you make in her.'

'That's only fair,' he said.

The fresh air had done her a power of good, Mike thought. She looked years younger, prettier too. And, joke title or not, she had brought her ship up some seriously tough miles of waterways, without a scratch. A woman who grew to match the challenges made on her — not unlike the redoubtable Ella, after whom Noel had named his boat. This woman would be an equal partner in any relationship.

The thought surprised him. 'Cast off,' he

said, and watched approvingly as she undid the neat knot, eased the bows of the boat from the bank, and stepped easily onto the narrow ledge around the cabin. 'Don't hang about there or you *will* need a hard hat,' he warned, smiling.

Becky realized she'd been staring at him. Ever since Bob had walked out on her, she had never taken up with another man. Too many responsibilities, with a child depending on her. Too many disappointments, from all the dreams with which they had started out. Too much hurt, from being rejected.

From that day until now, she had met men on her own terms — with a high, defensive wall between herself and them. What had kept her standing on the cabin ledge was a sudden realization. With Mike, she felt so safe and comfortable that she hadn't even bothered to set up that wall.

'Just thinking about the dinner I'm going to cook,' she said. 'And you're staying to share it with us this time. Because we will be moored in your yard.'

'Aye, aye, Cap'n,' he replied.

'I've a bottle of wine hidden somewhere,' Noel said.

'Not another one,' groaned Becky.

'Purely medicinal. The best doctors recommend a glass of wine, after going through a damp and smelly tunnel.'

'I'll drink to that,' said Mike. 'OK, here we go . . . '

He increased the revs and the *Ella Mae* slid gently into the tunnel. At first, their eyes struggled to adjust. Daylight became gloom, then darkest night. Ahead, their puny spotlights reflected off wet bricks on the tunnel roof.

It was spooky, claustrophobic. The noise from their engine beat back at them, while the tunnel air was thick with stale diesel fumes.

'Get into the cabin,' Becky ordered, as Jonathon began to cough.

'No,' he spluttered. 'Let me see. I promise not to cough.'

He broke his promise instantly.

'Hold this handkerchief to your nose and mouth,' Mike said.

In the gloom, she saw him pull out a handkerchief, still in its folds. He handed it to the boy, who held it over his mouth and nose.

'Better?' asked Mike.

Jonathon nodded. 'What's that light?' he asked. 'Is it the end of the tunnel already?'

'No, it's a breathing shaft. Goes up to the top of the hill above us — we'll pass three or four of them.'

For a moment, the gloom of the tunnel turned to smoky grey, then they were back in inky blackness again.

'Hope we don't meet anybody,' Becky said, her voice echoing.

'Plenty of room, if we do.' Mike replied. 'We just slow down, make sure our wash doesn't rock the other boat too much . . . it does the same for us.'

It was the longest mile of Becky's life, almost twenty minutes long. At last, a real glow showed at the end of the tunnel. The water of the canal in front of them turned grey, then silver, then molten gold.

They broke through into sunshine, Foulridge village all around them.

'Wow!' said Jonathon.

His eyes were beyond the village. Ahead, as far as Becky could see, there were rolling hills and green fields edged with dark trees, their spring leaf buds only starting to break into leaf. Then beyond the hill slopes, which the canal was hugging, rose tall blue hills.

'That's the Yorkshire Dales,' said Mike. 'They sweep down to the edge of the canal up north, as it turns into Airedale.'

'That's what I brought you both here to see,' said Noel. 'That's God's Own Country up ahead. Better than any pot of gold at a rainbow's end.' He smiled gently at Becky. 'That's where your future could lie.'

Becky looked at the great silent hills. Her chest tightened with emotion, until she thought she must cry. Then, gentle as an angel's kiss, a huge wave of joy engulfed her.

'*Our* future, Noel,' she whispered. 'A new future, for each and every one of us.' She turned blindly to him, reaching out, and hugged him. Then Jonathon.

'Me too?' asked Mike hopefully.

'You too,' she said, without a second's hesitation.

She hugged him, felt his gentle pat on her back in response.

Where it had touched, she tingled . . .

★ ★ ★

Kathy turned down her music and rose to go to the door. Who was calling this late at night? There was a spyhole set into the front door, but she never bothered to use it. As she opened the door, a gust of cold wind swirled in.

'Christine!' she said, surprised.

It was her ex-head teacher, her coat collar pulled high against the bluster of the night — so normal on this coast, that neither noticed it.

'Come in,' said Kathy, stepping back.

'If you don't mind. I won't take long.'

A surge of hope coursed through Kathy. Was she getting her job back? She led the older woman through into the living space, glad she had tidied things earlier that afternoon, out of habit rather than necessity.

'Can I get you a coffee? A glass of wine?'

'Coffee would be nice.' A slow smile came on Christine's face. 'You like your music,' she commented. 'I sense that your flat is built around it.'

Kathy grinned. 'My mum always said it was just as well I was born when CDs were in fashion. Back when everybody bought pop singles records, I'd have needed a bigger house to hold them. I'll get your coffee.'

She came back with the cafetiere and a couple of cups on a tray, with milk and sugar — neither of which she ever used herself — and a plate of elderly biscuits, which she prayed had not gone soggy. They felt firm enough. Snacking, or entertaining, were seldom part of Kathy's routine.

'Well, how can I help you, Christine?' she asked.

'I don't really have the right to ask . . . have you found another job yet?'

Promising.

'I'm applying for everything — but there's not much on offer. I'm working part-time at a local supermarket. I'd go mad, stuck in the flat all day.'

'I'm ever so sorry. With the funds to cover you, I would have kept both you and Rebecca on. Frankly, there are several members of staff I would have dispensed with first . . . but couldn't, given their terms of employment.'

Not so promising. Kathy's hopes began to wither on the vine. She sipped her coffee, trying to look bright and interested rather than depressed and angry.

Christine studied the biscuit collection: either it didn't come up to standard, or there was something else on her mind. 'I have no right to ask, but . . . ' she said.

'But what?'

'I can't think of any other way to solve the problem.'

'Which is?' Kathy was never given to small talk. Least of all, now.

'Do you remember our after-school Drama Club?'

'Of course. I helped to rehearse its last production.'

Christine sipped her coffee. 'We're in truly desperate straits, staff-wise,' she said. 'Obviously, there are no replacements for you or Rebecca. One other teacher off with stress-related problems. It leaves me three short, and everyone has had to take a share of the classes that are no longer covered. On top of a pretty full teaching load. People only see teaching as a 9 to 3.30 job. They never think about the hours of correction of the students'

72

work, or the nightly preparation of the lessons for the following day . . . '

She put down her cup with a double-click on the saucer. Kathy realized that the older woman's hands were shaking. More stress symptoms?

'To cut a long story short, Kathryn,' Christine said, 'nobody has time to set up and run the school play. For the first year since I took over, we won't have a show for parents in the summer. It's not a major tradition, but it means a lot to me — and to the children.'

'So?' asked Kathy.

'All I can think of is to ask a favour from someone who doesn't owe me any favours. Could you find the time at nights, to set up and organize some sort of play for the Drama Club? Then run rehearsals? I can't promise payment — although I will try my hardest to find some sponsorship. School funds are already stretched to breaking point . . . '

There was a long silence.

'Like I said, I have no right to ask you this . . . '

'OK,' said Kathy. 'It's a deal.'

She had enjoyed her involvement, last year. And the thought of working with kids again was exciting. 'I'd love doing that, Christine,' she added.

For a few moments, the lines of worry disappeared from the head teacher's face. 'My instinct told me that it was right for you,' she said. 'I would never have dreamed of asking, otherwise. You're a natural teacher. I want to keep in touch with you — and I want you to keep in touch with teaching — just in case we ever find the funds to bring you back.'

'And you'll give me a completely free hand?'

'Absolutely.'

'Enough funds to buy or hire a play?'

'Within reason.'

'And I can organize this exactly as I want to run it?'

A warm smile appeared on the older woman's face. Kathy's enthusiasm was catching. 'I have a feeling this could be a very special production,' she said.

'When do I start?' demanded Kathy.

★　★　★

Becky pulled aside the curtains, to look out onto a sunlit morning. She froze.

On the canal boat's window ledge was propped a mobile phone. Not hers — or Noel's. There was only one person it could belong to — Mike Preston. He must have left

74

it there over the meal, the night before. Probably to get a signal. And she had been so tired by night-time that she had simply made up her bed and fallen into it. Living and working in the open air cures all sleeping problems.

Carefully, she lifted it. 'Noel!' she called through. 'That phone number you've got for Mike — is it his mobile or his landline?'

The cabin door opened and Noel's head poked through. 'Mobile.'

Silently, she held up the phone.

'Oh,' Noel said. 'OK. We can look up his landline in a phonebook.'

'I'll be shopping in Longbank village this morning, there's bound to be a phone booth there. We need more coal . . . that little stove devours it. You're sure there's a coal merchant's here?'

'Yates,' Noel said. 'They're behind the canal-side warehouses. Go over the bridge, and follow the lane north for a couple of hundred yards. It's on the right — the business is run by a father and daughter.'

After breakfast, leaving the others to wash the dishes, Becky walked up the canal bank towards the bridge. It was a beautiful morning, misty sunshine, dew turning both grass and cobwebs into jewels. Beyond the village's neat houses, and the converted warehouse which was now office suites, the green fields and woods sloped ever upwards. Behind everything soared the blue hills of the Yorkshire Dales.

She drew in a lungful of crisp, cool air. God's Own Country indeed.

Becky climbed through the gate and onto the road bridge. She glanced up the canal as she walked across: half a dozen narrowboats, moored at decent intervals along the south bank, smoke rising lazily from some of the stovepipes, other boats clearly closed down.

She loved this gypsy way of life. Here today, and gone tomorrow. With no real plans beyond living each day fully, but one at a time. Her search for work must start after Skipton, down at Keighley and Bingley, perhaps even Bradford and Leeds. Somewhere, she hoped, there was a job waiting for her knock on the door — and near it, a decent school for Jon.

With a light step, she turned into the grey stone buildings of Joseph Yates and Son, Coal and Agricultural Merchants. A strange mix, she thought wryly. Noel had got it wrong: it was a son, not a daughter, who worked here.

In the cobbled yard outside the small, square office building, she hesitated. The place was deserted, no one in sight or sound. Pigeons fluttered down from a roof eave, startling her. Becky knocked on the battered and peeling office door.

No reply. She waited, then knocked again. Silence.

Not a problem, just an inconvenience. She could always come back later, after she'd picked up groceries from the village. By then, her arms would be full of plastic bags, her knuckles scraping the ground.

There had to be someone around, somewhere. She went to knock on the door again, then, on impulse, pushed against it instead. It creaked loudly, opening reluctantly on stiff hinges.

'Hello!' Becky called. 'Anyone in?'

No reply. She hesitated, and pushed the door further open.

An empty office, with ancient and rusting filing cabinets. Shelves piled high with stacks of paper, box files leaning drunkenly against them. What looked like a couple of old heating irons, holding the ends of the mess from sliding off. Walls thickly papered with all sorts of farming notices, yellowing, shredded corners, phone numbers scrawled across them and covered with black fingerprints.

A venerable wooden desk, only two or three peeling scabs of varnish remaining on its vertical surfaces. The desktop itself buried under office diaries, invoices, opened files with dirty smudges under the scribbled text. Behind it, a battered, leather-padded swivel chair, stuffing gaping through its back. Everything abandoned, like an experiment which had gone horribly and terminally wrong.

Becky was turning away, when the phone rang. The ringing was transmitted out into the yard, scattering the flock of pigeons.

Maybe somebody would come to answer it. Becky waited, hand on door.

The phone rang on and on. Stopped, then started up again.

On an impulse which she never understood, Becky went into the office, searched through the mess of papers and found the phone. She picked it up.

'Hello,' she said. 'I'm sorry. There's nobody here.'

'That caan't be true, lass,' a broad Yorkshire voice replied. 'Tha's answered it. Soombody must be there . . . Here's our order for t'week . . . '

'But,' protested Becky, 'I'm just . . . '

'Tell Henrietta we want twenty bags of t' usual, an' . . . '

'Twenty bags of what?'

'Animal feed. Thingie. Was on tip o' tongue, a minute ago.'

'Hold on . . . let me find some paper . . . a

biro . . . OK, who am I talking to?'

'Who else but me, lass? Tim Barnaby from Cobblestones, oop t'Dales.'

Becky nudged the phone into a more comfortable place between shoulder and ear, held down the sheet of invoice paper — already full on the other side — and began to write. 'Now,' she said. 'Give me your order. But slowly. I'm only passing by, and I haven't a clue what you're talking about.'

'You're doing reet fine,' the hearty voice replied. 'Champion. Now, here's order . . . give a shout, if I'm goin' too fast . . . '

The dictated list went on and on. Becky read it back to Barnaby, when it was finally completed. She had to amend a couple of items. She stared at it, as the phone clicked off. If that was a single farm, and this a regular order, then this strange, amalgamated business was likely to be busy after all.

She sat in the office chair, laid the borrowed biro down on the mess of papers, and looked at the order she had taken. How, out of the chaos which was piled high on the desk, was she going to bring this to the owner's attention? If she laid it down anywhere, it would instantly merge into anonymity amidst the other papers scattered there.

Sellotape it to the phone? Where, in this mess, would there be Sellotape?

79

Becky shuffled the piles of paperwork around. Nothing. Reluctantly, she gripped the handle of the top drawer. She didn't like this at all: it made her feel like a burglar. If anyone were to come in . . .

The doorway darkened.

Becky looked up to see a small, square woman, black with coal dust, a battered and scuffed leather apron strapped onto broad shoulders and back.

The two women stared at each other.

'Who the heck are you?' the coal-black figure demanded. 'And what the devil are you doing, raking through my desk? Step back, I'm going to phone the police.' Fearless eyes gleamed in the black and sweat-streaked face. 'Don't try to run,' she warned. 'You're nicked! Caught in the very act of stealing . . .'

4

'I am *not* a thief!' Becky said indignantly. 'I came here to buy coal. The place was deserted. When your phone rang, I tried to help. I was looking for Sellotape to stick this farmer's order onto your phone. Here!' she flicked the order form across the cluttered desk. 'It's yours — do what you want with it!'

She rose, pink-faced and furious. 'Now, better check your desk,' she said angrily. 'Make sure there's nothing missing, before I leave.'

A slow smile broke out on the coal-stained face. Absently, the woman picked up the order form and glanced at it. 'You write neat,' she said.

'And I don't steal.'

A coal-blackened hand waved placatingly. 'I hear you. Do you drink tea? I came in to make a brew and wash down t'dust.' The smile became a white-toothed grin, startling against the dirty face. 'That is, if I can find the kettle . . . a bit of a shambles, isn't it?'

A bit, Becky thought incredulously. 'On that shelf over there,' she pointed.

'So it is. There's a kitchen sink through in

the other room, if you want to fill t'kettle. I'll find a home for this.'

Becky lifted the plastic kettle and went through. It was more a cupboard than a kitchen, but was spotlessly clean and well organized. Maybe it was desk-work rather than untidiness which was the problem. She filled the kettle, found a socket and plugged in.

'Tea or coffee?' she called through.

'Tea. Black as it comes — and no sugar.'

Becky picked up two spotless mugs and busied herself. When she came through with a mug in each hand, she found the coal-woman sitting wearily at the desk, the order form still in hand.

'Sit down,' the woman said. 'Sorry, we got off on the wrong foot. My fault, jumping to conclusions. Henrietta is the name, Henrietta Yates. And you are?'

'Rebecca Calderwood.'

The older woman took the mug of scalding tea, and half-emptied its contents in a single gulp. 'That's better,' she sighed. 'You don't look like a Rebecca?'

'People call me Becky.'

'Good. Less frightening.'

'Less frightening!' Becky exclaimed. 'You come storming in through the door, and call me frightening?'

Again that lovely white-toothed grin. 'Well, you were. Sitting there, looking all posh and disapproving . . . '

'I couldn't find the Sellotape.'

'No more can I. It's been lost these last three months.' The rest of the mug was drained. 'I'm off to make another? Yourself?'

'I haven't even started.'

'Hang about. Won't be a second . . . ' For a few minutes there were busy noises and running water in the kitchen. When Henrietta came out, she was not only carrying a fresh mug of tea, but had also washed her face and hands and removed the coal-carrier's leather shield. 'No point in taking a bath or changing, until the deliveries are finished,' she excused. 'You said you wanted coal?'

'Two bags, please.'

'Where?'

'Down at the canal — the *Ella Mae*. We can bring her up to the bridge-side, and transfer the coal from there.'

With a sigh, Henrietta settled down in her leather chair. 'Let's get tea down us, first,' she said. She shuffled the littered papers with her free hand. 'I'm ashamed of this,' she admitted. 'Never was much good at paperwork. Broad shoulders and a weak brain. It was my dad who did the paperwork at nights. He wasn't much better, but we bumbled

through. Since he died, three months ago
. . . the whole place has sort of got away from
me.'

'I'm sorry,' Becky said automatically.

'About Dad? A real character. Could barely
read and write, let alone keep the books. But
he never landed us in prison, yet. I'm not sure
folks will be able to say the same about me.'

'Why don't you employ a bookkeeper?'
Becky asked.

'Not enough work for one. And we've
always kept business in t'family.'

'Fair enough — but why not get someone
in, to sort out this mess? Then start again?'

The light blue eyes grew thoughtful. 'We've
hired casual labour,' Henrietta nodded.
'Cover for emergencies, like. Can you hire a
bookkeeper like that?'

Becky shrugged. 'Don't know.'

Henrietta sipped tea, her eyes never leaving
Becky's. 'Are you passing through, or stopping?'
she finally asked.

'Stopping for a bit. Then heading down
through Skipton towards Keighley and Bradford. I need to find a job.'

A long silence.

'Ever kept books?'

'I'm a teacher — I was a teacher. Now I'm
looking for work.'

'And I'm offering. Three days a week, for

two weeks. Then we'll see where we are, and take it from there. Can't do full-time. But it would be good to have this mess cleared up.'

Becky was tempted. What had Noel said? *Take any sort of job, while you look for a better one. Any port in a storm.*

'I wouldn't know where to start,' she warned.

That wonderful flashing smile again. 'Neither do I!'

'I might make a right old cobblers of it.'

'I already have.'

Becky was warming to this woman — the most direct person she had ever met. 'I can only try,' she cautioned.

'That's good enough. A deal, then?'

'It's a deal.'

Henrietta rose from behind the desk. 'Up here we usually spit on our hands then shake them, to seal the deal,' she smiled. 'No written contracts ever. But I will waive the spitting bit for you.'

'Does that make it any less binding?' Becky laughed.

'Don't know. Only ever done it our way.'

Becky took a deep breath. 'OK,' she said, spitting on her hand. 'Why change the habits of a lifetime . . . ?'

★ ★ ★

Kathy went over to the classroom window. Evening was falling fast, and the empty school had all sorts of eerie noises — almost echoes of the generations of kids who had rioted through the place. She turned away, as the first of the four-by-fours rolled up, and three children got out. Restlessly, she flipped through her notes for the night ahead, although she already knew these off by heart.

She had forgotten how it felt to be a teacher — balancing on a high wire between exhilaration and pure stage fright. A real adrenalin buzz. She twitched, as more car doors slammed.

Would her idea work, she wondered. Giving the kids a few days, to read the plays' outlines and cast of characters, listen to the CDs of songs they would have to sing, then choose? A wry smile touched her lips. Christine was right: this would be a play with a difference.

Kathy was running on instinct. From last year's work with the Drama Club, she knew that the main problem was the tattered and stodgy play: written by an adult for adults to perform, then somehow cut down and put into short trousers by someone in education, for kids to take over the acting. Boring. At times, it had been like trying to flog a dead horse into life, getting the kids to believe in

86

what they were doing and show enthusiasm.

Culminating in a show which had — even more than usual — seemed only like people going through the motions. A stilted and pedestrian performance, followed by dutiful applause from parents and grandmothers.

It could all be so much better if you could spark, then harness, kids' interest and commitment. The internet was full of new plays and events, written specifically for kids. The three outlines and opening scenes she had selected from *Playz4kidz* were more musicals than plays, with lots of good ensemble numbers. Making minimal demands for sets and costumes, because the kids would mostly be playing themselves. And structured not simply for a leading lady and a leading man, but with everybody a hero, and an equal part. Saving all the squabbles and jostling from kids each of whom was treated as the Centre of the Universe at home.

But would it work? Could 10 and 11-year-olds take on the responsibility of choosing their own play, then throwing themselves into bringing it to life?

Kathy believed they could.

The Drama Club trooped in, a defensive bunch. Kathy did a quick mental head count. All present: they had gathered outside and come in gang-handed. As nervous of her as she was of them — maybe because they had never before had to take the responsibility for choosing their own play, then making that work.

She had organized the classroom so that everyone was sitting round a large discussion table, made up of desks. Not quite as round as King Arthur's from the legend, but with the same objective in mind: no obvious leaders.

'Well,' Kathy said briskly. 'Have you read the plays?'

A collective nod.

'And have you talked about which play you want to do?'

Lots of shifty side glances, then a reluctant nod.

'And?' Kathy waited, heart pounding.

Eyes studiously avoided any form of contact, with her or each other. The silence lengthened. This would never do . . .

'C'mon, guys!' she said. 'Somebody tell me what the others think.'

One of the older boys looked up. 'Do we call you *Miss?*' he asked.

Kathy gambled. 'It's outside school hours. We'll be working on this for weeks as a team together. So you can call me *Miss*, or you can call me Kathy — your choice. Let's vote on it. Right . . . how many for *Miss?*'

One small girl's hand went up, hesitated,

then crept back down again.

'How many for Kathy?' She wanted to cross her fingers and pray, because this was the crucial moment which would make or break the relationship she needed to forge with them.

After twenty racing heartbeats, one hand rose. The boy's, who had asked the question. Two others followed: his mates. Then, one by one, the others joined them. The small girl's hand the last to rise.

'Then Kathy it is,' she said briskly. 'Now tell me yours — there are three of you from last year's production, but I don't know the rest. You're Donald,' she said, pointing. 'And you keep forgetting your lines . . .'

This brought a rueful grin. 'They were boring, Miss.'

'Kathy.'

'Well, they were . . . Kathy. Nothing like these plays you gave us to look at.'

'Cool,' said the first boy. 'I'm Jim. All the new plays are dead brilliant.'

Suddenly, the room was filled by a chorus of voices — the children's names and the merits and demerits of the three plays all shouted at the same time. Kathy heaved a sigh of relief. She could pick up the kids' names later. The important thing was that the ice was broken, and they liked her choice of plays.

'OK, OK,' she called, waving down the volume. 'So are you going to vote for which play we will buy to rehearse?'

'No need. We've chosen it.'

'And it's?'

'*Almost-But-Not-Quite-Happy Families* . . . it's great.'

'Anybody against?' she asked. Firm head-shakes all round. 'Fine, why did you pick that one?'

'It's like seriously cool.'

'It's dead funny . . . '

'It's about kids just like us . . . '

'They're like our family — and I want to be the family dog.'

'The songs are great — can I bring my guitar?'

'Hold on,' laughed Kathy. 'Have you sorted out who is going to play which character yet? Or do you all want to be the same one?'

'I want to be the family dog, Kathy. It's only fair, I asked first.'

'Does anybody else want to be the family dog?' Kathy asked.

Head-shakes all round.

'Well, we've cast our first character,' sighed Kathy. 'Now we'd better get down to sorting out the rest . . . '

★ ★ ★

'Where's Becky?'

Noel looked up from his book, to see a coal-smudged face peering down into the cabin from the steering well.

'She's gone off to Foulridge in the bus,' he replied. 'You're Henrietta?'

'How did you guess?'

'I'm psychic. Plus the coal dust is a bit of a giveaway.'

A startlingly white grin split the dirty face. 'On Mondays and on Tuesdays, it's coal. So I'm black from head to foot. On Wednesdays through to Saturdays, it's farmstuff, so I'm white with grain and animal-feed dust. The only time I see my own skin is nights and mornings. Where do you want the coal?'

'In the bunker here. If you hand down . . .'

'Look, I was carrying coal for my dad, when I was still in nappies — just give me space to fetch it through.'

The small square figure was much more nimble than Noel expected. She came quickly down into the cabin, reached up to take a fistful of coarse bag in each hand, then grunted. The canal boat rocked slightly, as she lifted the bag from the top of the steps and carried it by arm strength alone through the cabin to the bunker at the side of the stove.

'Tally-ho,' she said, emptying the coal. 'One more, to go.'

When she was finished, she folded the dirty bags up in the steering well.

'How much do I owe?' Noel asked.

'Nothing. That's an advance on Becky's wages.'

'Ah. She said you'd given her a job, to clear up your paperwork.'

'That's putting it mildly,' Henrietta smiled. 'It's a bulldozer she needs to get started. Well, I'm off. Who's the boy down in the cabin?'

'Jonathon. Becky's son.'

'What's he doing there? Drawing? On holiday?'

'He's doing his schoolwork, as set by his mum. She's a teacher.'

'So she said. Was she a good 'un?'

'If conscientious is good, then she's good. If breaking the material down into under-standable soundbites for a child is good, then she's good. And if keeping Jon's nose to the grindstone until he finds a new school is good . . . '

'OK. I get the message. She's good. Could be interesting . . . '

An experienced reporter, Noel simply tilted his head: people say more, when they're talking freely, than they ever do in answer to a question. He became aware that Henrietta was watching him sardonically.

'Think I came floating down the canal in a

biscuit barrel?' she demanded.

He shrugged. 'I was waiting to hear what you were going to say.'

'Not yet. Need to think on it.' Henrietta's smile disappeared. 'You used to come through here regular,' she said. 'I've loaded coal into this boat before.'

'I've had a brainwave,' said Noel. 'How about us playing this game? You be the ruthless tabloid journalist, and I will be the victim . . .'

Henrietta threw back her head and laughed. 'Well it's true, isn't it? I never forget a face, or an order. But I haven't seen you around here in years. You used to pass through, with a . . .' Her eyes widened, as realization dawned. 'Oh, I'm sorry . . . it's your wife, isn't it? She's gone now? It's the one thing we do well, up here in Yorkshire . . . open our mouth, then stick both feet in it.'

'It's all right,' Noel said. 'I lost Ella three years ago. I've been a bit like old Queen Victoria, I think — let my mourning period go on too long, until it took over and nearly ruined my life.'

'That's the danger,' said Henrietta. 'I've just lost my dad.'

She sniffed, and cuffed her face. Leaving a new white smear against the black smudges on her cheek. 'There's only ever been my dad and me, since I was a tiny kid. Leaves a gaping, Dad-sized hole beside you,' she said unsteadily. 'Takes a bit of getting used to, don't it?'

'That hits the nail on the head,' said Noel quietly. 'I was just going to put the kettle on . . . fancy a cup of tea?'

'I'd leave a mucky trail behind me.'

'I can clean it up, so she'll never know.'

'Becky? Would take more than a mucky trail to annoy that one. But it's a nice day, spring's heading north. We could sit out here and sip our brew.'

'I'd like that,' Noel said. 'I'll get the kettle going.'

Henrietta hesitated, then sat down on one of the canvas bags — at least she could see where the worst muck was on that, and fold it inside. The cabin door opened, and the boy came shyly out.

'You're Jonathon,' she said.

'Nobody ever calls me that.'

'Then I will.'

Jonathon hesitated. 'Noel sent me to interview you,' he apologized. 'Mum's set me a project of finding out the history of every place we stop at for more than a couple of nights. I was going up to the library tomorrow. But Noel says that people always know more interesting stuff than books. So can you tell me, please, what do you know about Longbank's history?'

'Well, you're a one!' Henrietta said, taken aback.

'C'mon, your family have been here for generations,' Noel's voice came through. 'Do you take milk and sugar in your tea?'

'I take it black. No sugar neither.' Henrietta glanced up the canal to the village. 'My dad always said that we were the most important wharf on the whole canal. He said the canal boats brought up coal from Burnley and Blackburn, and cotton goods from Liverpool and Manchester. Then they tipped their loads on the wharf here, and we hauled it up into the Dales. Then we filled our wagons with the raw wool from the Dales up north and loaded that into the canal boats, for them to ship down to the mills in Bradford and Leeds. Then the canal people collected all the woven woollens and worsteds, and took them back through us and down to Liverpool and the west. And the wool that was grown in the Dales here — up on these hills back there — that went all round the world from the Port of Liverpool.'

Noel emerged through the doorway, a steaming mug in each hand. 'See!' he told Jonathon. 'People are always more interesting than books.'

★ ★ ★

After following her instinct and bringing back Mike's mobile phone, Becky's courage ran out. She hesitated outside his office, before knocking.

'Come in.'

The words were said absently, as if his mind was on something else.

Becky pushed open the door. 'So this is your domain?' she said, glancing round the neat shelves and the technical drawings pinned on every wall, and thinking that the office reflected the man. Calm, uncluttered and somehow understated — at the opposite end of the scale from Henrietta's nightmare den.

Mike rose from where he had been working on repair estimates.

'This is where it happens,' he said cheerfully. 'Or at least where it's meant to happen. Thanks for bringing back my moby. I leave a trail of things behind — it drives everybody mad. But I could easily have nipped up and collected it tomorrow.'

'By tomorrow, I will be working,' Becky smiled. 'Part-time. In a coal yard.'

She was glad she had trusted her instinct. She liked this easy-going giant, and sensed that she could like him a whole lot more. Pity they would soon be moving on, but she was happy just to live for the day, like any canal family.

'Will you be carrying bags of coal?' he teased.

'My new boss does,' Becky laughed. 'She's brought me in to sort out the mess of paperwork. Everything's so neat, both here and in your workshop.'

'That's my granddad's long shadow. In his day, every tool had its own place on the wall. And the first job in my apprenticeship with him was to learn the name and the uses of each single tool.'

'I thought you were a football player?'

'My dad made me finish my apprenticeship — in case my football career went pear-shaped. It's a tough physical sport, and we all know the risks.'

'Good thinking — but didn't you resent that at the time?'

Mike ran fingers through his unruly hair. 'It's so long ago . . . but I don't think there was any clash. All I ever wanted to do was what my family did — work on boats. We've been here for three generations, and I can trace back my roots to full-time canal families on both sides — to real Romanies, in one of them. Canals are in our blood. Football was only a diversion.'

He led her out through the office door. 'Come on, I'll give you the full guided tour. All three minutes' worth. You've seen the office. I'll show you round my workshop and the Wharf, to see the narrowboats I'm working on.'

'A one-man business?'

'In the summer months, when everybody's wanting repairs done yesterday, and the hire firms are wanting me to look at problems their own fitters can't solve, sure, I could use some extra hands to help me out. It's dawn to dusk and longer, then. But for eight months of the year, there's only full-timers on the waterways and a steady trickle of work from folk like Noel, who have used us all their lives.'

'There can't be many like Noel, who knew all three generations?'

'You'd be surprised. We've a good name, and I mean to keep it that way — we're not going from clogs to clogs in three generations on my watch. Not after the hard work and sacrifice by my dad and granddad.'

This was another side to his personality, she thought.

'So your family started up the business?' she asked.

'They took it over. My granddad gambled everything, sold up his two boats and borrowed from the local bank, to buy the yard when its owner died. He worked here all his life, paying off that loan at a few pounds a month. The banks were your friends back then, and stood by you. When my dad took over, the freight-carrying business was dead on its feet — everything was going by road and rail. We were in a state of collapse, with some of the original loan still outstanding.'

His voice was quiet, but she could sense how deeply he felt about the yard and the generations who had gone before him.

'What turned things round?' she asked.

Mike stared over the moored narrowboats. 'Things hit rock bottom in the seventies. All the old working boats were abandoned, some left to sink and rust or rot in the canal. The banks fell in, the waterway silted up. Then a bunch of enthusiasts who had helped in reclamation work down south started hounding the Water Board and local governments into rescuing the Leeds and Liverpool.'

He looked down at her: her face was serious, eyes intent and a slight furrow of concentration on her brow. She was interested, he decided, and not just making small talk. The slight breeze had drifted some of her hair across her face. He wanted to reach out and sweep it back.

'You'll make it, you know,' he said gently. 'The job and everything.'

Becky blinked, taken aback. 'How do you know?'

He smiled. 'How do you know, before you even step onto a new canal boat, that she's a good 'un? I just *know*.'

'Let's hope you're right. But what finally rescued the canal?'

'When the waterway was restored, people began to use it,' Mike said. 'Not working boats, but leisure sailors. For ten to fifteen years there was an explosion of work in converting the old hulls into narrowboat cruisers, like the *Emma Mae*. I'm glad my granddad saw his dream finally realized. He was over eighty by then, and still the best fitter on the canal. He saw us worked off our feet, by conversions and repairs, and making money for the first time.'

'So why are you back to being a one-man business?'

'I like it that way. It's a choice of lifestyle, as much as a job.'

'And you never miss the bright lights?'

'Not ever. It's so much better here.'

'Is that why Noel calls this God's Own Country?'

He smiled. 'He's a Scotsman, and we Yorkshire tykes are the nearest you can get to that.'

'If you mean direct and down to earth, I agree. From what I've seen, I like the people and the place. I'm Scottish too, was brought up in Perth until my dad moved south with his job. I feel at home here.'

'That's good,' he said. There was something in this woman that touched him deeply. Simply standing here and talking to her made the day seem brighter.

'I usually have a cup of tea around now,' he said. 'Like to join me?'

'That would be nice. But I can't hang about too long. My bus back to Longbank goes through the village in forty minutes' time.'

'I'll run you home,' said Mike. 'So long as you don't mind travelling in a Transit van.'

'Why should I? But what about your office? Your work?'

'I'll ask my CEO,' Mike said solemnly. He tilted his head. 'He says it's OK.'

'Then you must have a very understanding boss.'

'One of the best,' agreed Mike. 'We seldom quarrel.'

'OK,' said Becky. 'You can drive me home on one condition. You will stay and have supper with us tonight.'

'I'd only leave my mobile there again . . . '

'Then I'd have to bring it back tomorrow. After work.'

'And I'd have to run you home again . . . on headlights.'

Becky laughed. It had been years since she had felt this happy.

'Wouldn't it be easier in the long run, if I caught the bus?' she demanded.

Mike smiled down, grey eyes twinkling in a face tanned dark by weather: 'Yes. But it wouldn't be half the fun.'

'OK, you win,' said Becky. 'But I'm taking the bus home tomorrow night . . . or we could spend the whole summer travelling up and down to Longbank.'

'I could think of worse ways to spend a summer,' Mike said quietly.

She registered his change of mood. 'Me too,' she smiled.

Thinking that it had been years since she had felt so alive, and young. And enjoying — indeed taking huge pleasure from — the company of a man.

★ ★ ★

They had just finished the second week of rehearsals, and the clamour of excited children's voices had gradually diminished as parents collected them. The read-through had gone well and they were planning to tackle the first two ensemble songs the following week.

Kathy felt drained but contented. Running

rehearsals single-handed was demanding, but the enthusiasm which the kids generated made them easy to control. Her main problem was holding them back, not coaxing them to perform.

She was left with Sally, by far the quietest of the bunch. And the janitor hovering in the doorway, willing them to go, so that he could lock up the building and head home.

'Dad's usually here, Miss,' Sally said, looking worried. 'He's always waiting outside, when we finish.'

'He'll have been held up in the traffic. And it's Kathy, remember?'

'Yes, Miss.'

This was the same little girl who had voted for Miss rather than her Christian name, and was still too shy to change her mind. Kathy sighed inwardly: you can't win them all. 'Don't worry. I'll wait with you until he turns up. If we stand at the school gates, that will let the janitor lock up.'

With a gentle hand on the girl's shoulder, she steered her outside.

'I'll never learn my part,' Sally said miserably. 'There's so many words.'

'Of course you will. We'll be over them so many times in rehearsal, you'll be saying them in your sleep. Have you acted in a play before?'

'No, Miss.'

'Kathy.'

'Yes, Miss.'

'Well, don't worry about it. You'll never be on stage on your own, there will always be somebody else there. Somebody inside you. Some of our greatest actors are always a bundle of nerves before the show. Can't learn their lines, no matter how they try. But when they go out on stage, a strange thing happens — they become the character they're playing, and all the words that they thought they couldn't remember come pouring out of them. Because the character takes over, and he or she has been listening inside, all the time. They know the words, even if you keep forgetting them.'

'And I can't sing either.'

'You'll all be singing together. Nobody is expecting you to sound like a pop star. The play's all about children, children talking, children singing. So long as you can make some sort of noise — squeak, even . . . '

At last, she broke through. Sally gave a gurgle of laughter.

'Like a little mouse?' she asked.

'Like a musical little mouse . . . squeaking in tune. *Squeak, squeak!*'

Kathy's put-on falsetto squeak turned the gurgle into a real laugh.

'I can do better than that,' Sally said.

'Bet you can't!'

'I can.'

'Then show me — and I'll tell you if your squeak is better than mine.'

In the dusk, a dark car slid in to the pavement beside them and stopped.

'It's Daddy!' said Sally.

'I still want that squeak,' Kathy demanded.

'*Squeak!*' It was a very small squeak.

'That was only a baby squeak,' laughed Kathy. 'Now, do me a proper one.'

'SQUEAK! SQUEAK!'

'That's more like it,' said Kathy.

She turned to see the tall figure of a man climb out of the car.

'We're rehearsing, Daddy,' Sally said. 'Wasn't my squeak better than hers?'

'I haven't heard hers, so I can't pass judgement,' the man smiled. 'Sorry I'm late, I had a puncture. Had to change to the spare. My hands are filthy . . . '

He held up his hands for them to see, but it was too dark.

'Thanks for staying with her, Miss,' he said.

'Kathy's her name. But she can't squeak as good as me.'

The man was walking round the front of the car. At the name, he stopped, and stared through the gloom.

'Kathy?' he said. 'Is that really you, Kathy? I've been looking everywhere for you . . . for days.'

She froze, goose pimples rising on her neck and across her shoulders.

'David!' she said. 'I didn't recognize you, out of a tracksuit.' Her heart seemed to stop beating, for several seconds. 'What on earth are you doing here?'

'Collecting my daughter,' he said quietly.

'Your daughter?' whispered Kathy. 'I didn't even know that you were married . . . '

5

'You ran away, before I could explain,' David said. 'Yes, I was married, but . . . '

'Mum died,' said Sally quietly. 'In a car crash.'

'Not her fault — she was the innocent victim,' said David.

'I'm so sorry,' Kathy stammered. 'I had no idea . . . '

'Of course not. Why should you? Where's your car?'

'I don't have one. I'm one of nature's pedestrians.'

'Then can I run you home? After all, you stayed behind with Sally.'

This guy was seriously nice, thought Kathy. For days, she had been trying to get over her embarrassment, put him out of her head, but without success. Now she could see why. Go with the flow, and see what developed, she decided.

'That would be nice,' she said. 'I'll sit in the back.'

'That's Sally's territory, She still needs a booster seat to be safe. Sit up-front and direct me back to your place.'

'I'm warning you,' said Kathy. 'I only know the bus routes.'

'There's no hurry,' David smiled, in the dusk. 'Come on, Sally. Climb onto your throne, and I'll fasten your seat belt.'

'I can do that myself!'

'Yes, I know. But just in case. Hop in, Kathy. Won't be a second . . . '

It was lovely and warm in the car — at least she hoped it was that, and not that she was blushing. I'm far too old to blush, thought Kathy, tucking some stray hair behind her ears.

'OK, where to?' asked David, dropping onto the seat beside her.

'Down to the end of the road, and turn right. Into John Street from there, then follow the Ormskirk signs. I'll tell you when to turn off again . . . '

As he eased his car into the traffic, David glanced across. 'I even went round some supermarkets, looking for you,' he confessed.

'We've got enough shopping to last us for a month,' came from behind.

David winced. 'You never told me you were still working part-time at teaching,' he said.

'I wasn't. This came out of the blue. I grabbed it with both hands.'

He nodded. 'Every penny helps, when you're out of work.'

'Not this time. The Head scraped up some sponsorship, but we're using that to rent performance rights. It was only a couple of hundred, anyway.'

David frowned. 'So you're doing this for nothing?'

'I like working with kids.'

'It's a great play,' said Sally from behind. 'It will be mega.'

'That's because I've got good actors,' said Kathy. 'Turn left, here.'

David turned into Kathy's street. 'OK, where's your flat?'

'Just after that white car.' Kathy got out, hesitated, then leaned back through the doorway. 'Coming in for coffee?' she asked. 'By way of me saying thanks?'

'Yes, please,' said Sally, as David hesitated.

Kathy looked at him, the query still in her eyes.

He smiled. 'The Boss has spoken. So long as we're not too much trouble.'

'None at all.' Kathy ran lightly up the steps and opened the door, praying that her fiat was tidy. She switched on the lights, and glanced around. When you live alone, things tend to get put down and forgotten. But the flat was fine.

'Tea or coffee?' she asked over her shoulder.

'Coffee, please,' David replied, ushering a wide-eyed Sally before him. She moved, as if pulled by strong magnets, to the shelves where Kathy kept her CD collection — floor to ceiling — along two walls. 'Don't touch!' he warned.

'Let her be . . . ' Kathy's voice came from the kitchen.

David walked through to stand in the kitchen doorway.

'She's music mad,' he said. 'Like her mum was. Beth played in the Liverpool Philharmonic. But she loved folk, jazz, Celtic music — anything.' He paused. 'Sally is why I couldn't come for a meal,' he said awkwardly. 'I'm all she's got. She's still so insecure, that even when she's at home, she keeps coming through to check that I'm still there. We lost her mum two full years ago, but Sally's never really recovered.'

'I understand,' said Kathy.

Their eyes locked.

'However, I do want to see you again,' David said quietly. 'For the first time since Beth died, I genuinely want to see someone else. After I recognized this, I can say it without feeling guilt. When you asked, I still hadn't got that bit clear in my mind. So, if I could replay that conversation, it would be to say: Yes, Kathy, I would like to have a meal with you . . . but at my place, with Sally, where I'll do the cooking and fill you with cold rice pudding. Then I'll run you into the ground next morning, when I'm free to go anywhere I want.'

Kathy's heart was pounding. 'OK. Consider the conversation wound back and rerun.'

'And?'

'Let's do it. The cold rice pudding was always optional.'

David grinned. 'That's how crooked handlers try to slow down greyhounds, don't you know?' he accused her.

'Do I look like someone who would slow down a grey-hound?' Kathy demanded.

'No. But you wouldn't hesitate with a competitor.'

'That's different,' said Kathy. 'I love dogs.'

'That puts me in my place. Can I wash my hands?' David held up his hands, black with the dirt from changing his wheel for the puncture.

'You can do it posh, in the loo, or here in the kitchen sink. Feel free.'

'Then I'll mess up your kitchen,' he said cheerfully, and paused.

From the front room came the sounds of music. Billie Holiday, at her most smoky-voiced, singing through an old blues number.

'We'll never get Sally home now,' he sighed.

Kathy handed him his coffee. 'OK,' she said. 'How shall we do this meal? Share the cooking? You provide the main course, and I'll bring the pudding?'

David laughed. 'I have a better idea,' he said. 'I'll cook both courses.'

'It's a deal,' said Kathy.

She tilted her head, listening to the music. 'Is she into good jazz?'

'Like her mum, everything musical.'

'How about Charlie Parker?'

'The jazz saxophonist?'

'The world's greatest ever jazz saxophonist,' Kathy corrected.

'If you say so.'

'I've a CD of his somewhere. It's a perfect introduction to him. If there's music in her soul, then he'll reach out and claim her as his own.'

★　★　★

'I must be in the wrong place,' Henrietta said. 'This used to be my office!' Her cheerful face was covered in white dust, streaked with sweat channels — it was an agricultural feedstuffs day.

'Very funny,' said Becky. 'All I've done is sort out the mess on your desktop into different piles — like invoices, order forms, final demands from the gas and electricity . . . '

'Final demands?' asked Henrietta. 'Where did you find these?'

'Under the mess.'

'Ah,' said Henrietta. 'That's why I didn't see them.'

Becky sighed. 'Now, all we have to do is write invoices to the customers whose orders you've been delivering. Then write cheques to cover the bills from all your suppliers. Then think up a convincing excuse, and phone the gas and electricity people. Finally, when we've sorted out the paperwork, maybe I can start to bring your books up to date. When did you last write them up?'

Henrietta stared at the wall, hoping for inspiration. 'You've taken down all my wall-calendar thingies!' she exclaimed indignantly. 'I'd customers' names on these!'

'Your wall calendars were five years old. Some of the names on them have probably gone for good — and the rest you've got in your filing cabinet.'

'Have I?' asked Henrietta, having the grace to look surprised. Better to change the topic to a safer one, she decided. 'Fancy a mug of tea?'

'I'll make it. You phone the gas and

electricity people — before the bailiffs come and take away your kettle and your tea bags.'

'I'd like to see them try!'

'I'd rather we didn't give them the chance. Go on, the phone number is written out on each final notice. Your credit card is lying beside them.'

'My credit card? I've been looking all over for it! Where did you . . . ?'

'Your desk. Under the mess.'

'Then at least it wasn't lost. Right, you make the tea. I'll go and wash my face, before I phone them.'

'They can't see you. Phone them now.'

Henrietta sighed. 'We had a teacher once, just like you.'

'Did you drive her mad, as well?'

Henrietta's face lit up with that wonderful smile: 'Probably.'

Becky filled the kettle, hearing her boss chatting, laughing and talking credit card numbers into the phone. She smiled. It wasn't just the canal which flowed slowly here below the Dales. Even final demands seem to be settled at a more leisurely pace.

She carried through their tea.

'Cheers,' said Henrietta. She took her mug and gulped. 'That's better.'

Sitting down on the edge of the now-clear desk, she picked up an invoice from the neat

114

pile at Becky's side.

'Don't!' said Becky. 'They're all in order.'

'The place has lost its homely feel,' Henrietta complained. 'Now it's just like any other office in the world. No personality.'

'No mess,' corrected Becky.

Henrietta stuck out her tongue, then gulped down the rest of her tea. 'I'm off to make another brew. Want one?'

'No, thanks. There's another mug, ready to drink, in the kitchen. Cooling down for you.'

'How did you know I'd need it?'

'Because you always finish the first in two gulps.'

'Good thinking,' said Henrietta. 'That boy of yours. When are you sending him back in school?'

Becky was caught out by the sudden change of tack. 'As soon as I find a settled job myself.'

'Where?'

Becky shrugged. 'Wherever. Once I'm finished here, we'll probably move on . . . '

She didn't like the thought. If they swung east to Bradford, they would move away from Mike Preston's boatyard. Somehow, that was more of an issue than it should be. She was in no hurry to confront that day.

'Why not put him into school here?'

'You've got a school? A primary?'

'The Cluny Foundation. A small independent school.'

'I can't afford fees.'

'Locals get for free.'

'We're not locals.'

'You are, while you're staying here.'

Becky frowned. Jonathon's education was a worry. He was working well under her own teaching, but sooner or later the Education Authority would get restless. Kids educated at home cause nosebleeds in any bureaucratic system. 'I doubt that your school would see us as locals,' she muttered.

'They'll see whatever the chairman tells them.'

'Who's he?'

'It's a she. And you're looking at her.'

Henrietta savoured Becky's surprise.

'I'm not just a pretty face,' she said smugly. 'The Foundation's our school, and we run it our way, just like we've done for years. There's no Fancy Dans on our board — just local people. The school that Old Cluny built up and left has sent generations of our kids to college and university. That's good enough for us.'

'Does it teach the standard curricula?' Becky asked doubtfully.

'To a high standard. And everything else he brought back from his missionary work in Asia — the tolerance of different religions and cultures, understanding different societies, how they work, looking at our responsibilities within our own society. All the fancy stuff modern educators have only just discovered — we've been teaching it for a hundred years.'

Becky tried to focus on basics. 'You're telling me that it's a proper school, and that you can get Jonathon into it.'

'Exactly.'

'What if we have to move on in a month or so?'

'Let's worry about that in a month or so.'

'And you can definitely fit him in?'

'I told that Noel of yours that I would think about it. Well, I have.'

'Are you serious?'

'Cross my heart, and I don't tell lies,' chanted Henrietta.

'Well . . . ' said Becky, lost for words.

'Close your mouth, an' you'll catch no flies . . . ' Henrietta finished her somewhat mangled quotation.

★   ★   ★

'Anybody at home?'

Becky glanced up from her paperwork in Henrietta's office, to see Mike Preston standing in the doorway — so tall, he had to dip his head.

'What are you doing here?' she asked, her heart lifting.

'Passing through. I've been working all morning on one of the hire-fleet's engines at Skipton, and decided to drop in.' He looked around. 'Where's the mess you were talking about?'

'It's taken three days to clear. Want a mug of tea? Henrietta wouldn't grudge it.'

'Heart of gold, that woman. Renowned for it. She's been heaving coal for her dad since she was a girl. Missed half her schooling, helping out. Her mother died, when she was young, leaving only him and her. The old man used to laugh and tell folks that it was always a son he'd wanted — that's why he called her Henrietta — but once his daughter joined him, he was glad he had no sons.'

'Then why is it Yates and Son?' asked Becky.

'Her dad was the son. They've been carriers for generations.'

Becky rose to fill the kettle. 'She's chairman of the school board for the local school — did you know that?'

'No, but I'm not surprised. Don't let her paperwork fool you — that's one sharp businesswoman. Got a good head on her shoulders. She sees through to the root of a problem in seconds, and knows just as

118

quickly how to tackle it. She has a good brain — just never had the chance to educate it. She's perfect for their oddball school. What they need is an independent, clear-headed street fighter who fears nobody in Education, and Henrietta was born to do that job.'

Becky poured boiling water into the mugs. 'Why an oddball school?' she asked.

'The man who set it up, Joshua Cluny, was a retired missionary. He'd spent his life out East — India, China, Burma — and came back saying his congregations taught him more than he taught them. He set up his Foundation with money he got from Asian merchants, to coach their kids for public schools in England. Then he used the money from course fees to teach local kids for free.'

'But has it a good reputation?'

'Top drawer. It's as good as any fee-paying school — even if there are only a couple of teachers and about twenty-five kids.'

Becky sipped her tea. 'She's offered to take in Jon for a bit.'

'Grab it. You couldn't do better for him.'

'I could tell the education authorities that he's back in school.'

'Go for it!'

'Yes, but . . . '

The calm eyes studied her; she felt colour rise to her cheeks.

'But what?' he finally asked.

'Becky set down her mug. 'I'm not sure. Yes, I am. I'm scared that he'll be bullied again — he's been a different boy since I started teaching him on his own.'

'So that's been a problem, in the past?'

Becky nodded. 'He's small for his age, and shy. Kids pick on him.'

Mike strolled to the open door, mug in hand. 'Kids pick on anyone who doesn't quite fit in,' he said thoughtfully. 'They always have. So the trick would be to help him fit in quickly.' He turned. 'Does he play football?'

'No,' she said. 'No sports at all.'

Mike came over. 'I coach kids in Burnley and Blackburn — got all the certificates, and police clearance.' He pulled a face. 'You need that nowadays. I could bring over a ball and get him to kick it around. See what his co-ordination and sports skills are like.'

'Not sure I follow,' said Becky.

Mike grinned. 'Kids up here are football daft. Football and cricket. If a boy plays either sport well, it's his passport to being accepted. Trust me, I've had this problem before — lots of times. Most kids are clueless. So with a few hours of proper coaching, he'd be a star.'

His eyebrow rose. 'Worth trying?'

'I'd try anything,' Becky said. 'I just don't

want him miserable again.'

'Won't happen. I'll check him out tomorrow.'

'I can't pay you for coaching,' she said, shamefacedly.

'Who mentioned payment?'

'Then you'll have dinner with us? Before or after?'

'Let me put him through his paces, first.'

She rose to thank him, then, suddenly, they were standing very close.

The quiet grey eyes studied her, a slight frown on his serious face.

Then, slowly, he reached down and kissed the tip of her nose.

He blinked. 'Sorry,' he said. 'Didn't mean to . . . shouldn't have done that . . . no offence meant, Becky. I apologize.'

Her heart was beating loudly and steadily.

'And so you should,' she said. 'Call that a kiss?'

Running purely on instinct, she lifted her arms and reached up to him. 'If you're going to kiss a woman . . . then do it properly,' she said.

★　★　★

The meal at David's place had gone supremely well.

121

'Not often you get a runner who can cook,' complimented Kathy. 'Most of us simply swallow protein to feed our energy levels. Good cooking's dangerous — it adds on weight.'

'Daddy ran for the UK,' Sally said proudly. 'He ran in the Olympic Games.'

'That was a hundred years ago,' said David. 'And I came in last.'

'He didn't!' Sally turned to Kathy. 'He always lies about his running. He made the final and came in fourth.'

'As good as last.'

'Beaten only by the three greatest runners in the world,' his daughter insisted.

'Don't listen to her,' David smiled.

Kathy was staring at him. 'What distance?'

'Five thousand and ten thousand metres,' answered Sally. 'And he had to pull out of the second final, because he hurt his leg.'

'The only way I could think of getting out of it . . . '

'All lies,' said Sally. 'He came home limping. And he limped for weeks. He tore a hamstring, trying to match the final sprint of the others.'

Kathy found herself staring, her mouth half-open. She closed it with a click. 'And I had the . . . effrontery . . . to challenge you to a race?'

'Which you nearly won,' he smiled.

'Which I *did* win,' Kathy said indignantly.

David half-rose from the table, eyes twinkling. 'Why don't we go out and settle the question once and for all . . . '

Kathy groaned. 'I couldn't raise a trot, after that dinner.'

Sally's eyes had gone back and forwards in the good-humoured exchange, a slow smile growing on her face. 'Kathy?' she asked. 'Can I play you some of my music?'

'I'd love to hear your music,' Kathy said.

As the little girl ran through for a disc, David sighed. 'I better warn you,' he said. 'She has a very adult take on music. Her mother taught her well.'

Through the open door from the dining room, they heard a full orchestra play a gentle, sweeping introduction: very modern, sensual music. Then out of the rich colour of the different instruments a clear soprano voice came soaring. The words were German, Kathy guessed, but the beauty of the music was such that she didn't even try to translate them. She listened, goose pimples rising on her shoulders, captivated by the blending of voice and orchestra.

When the track finished, she felt something akin to pain at its loss.

'What on earth was that?' she asked. 'I have never heard anything so beautiful . . . not in all my life.'

Sally glanced at her father.

'It's your music. You tell her.'

'It's called *September*,' Sally said quietly. 'A love song written by an 80-year-old composer, in memory of his dead wife who'd been an opera singer. It is the third of Strauss's *Four Last Songs*. When he finished, he set his pen down and never composed another piece. He said he'd used up everything he knew, and felt, in these four songs.'

She glanced shyly across the table: 'Would you like to hear another?'

'Absolutely,' said Kathy.

The little girl scuttled out. A few seconds later, she was back, standing in the open doorway. 'Close your eyes,' she said. 'It helps you listen — I always close my eyes to hear the music properly.'

It would be impossible to surpass the first, Kathy thought. Then her hair stood on end as incandescently beautiful music came floating through. Ancient church music, written to be chanted by the dark voices of monks, with a boy's clear soprano soaring high above them into an impossibly beautiful phrase of melody.

'I know that,' Kathy whispered. 'It's the *Allegri Miserere*, isn't it? The one they used as theme music for Le Carre's *Tinker Tailor Soldier Spy*?'

She listened to the second verse, then the

third, her throat constricting each time the boy's soprano line soared free of the men's voices.

'Well?' Sally asked.

'Stunning,' Kathy replied. 'It's my most favourite piece.'

'Do you know its history?' Sally asked.

'Pass,' said Kathy. 'Tell me. Please.'

'When it was written hundreds and hundreds of years ago, the Church decided that it was too dangerous, too emotional, for people to hear. So they hid it away in a vault. They played it once, each year, in Rome, to an audience of a few invited people. Then hid it away again. But one year, a father and son were invited to listen. They were both composers and when they came out, the father tried to hum the melody, but kept drifting off it at the same place. The son said: 'If you like it, then I'll write it out for you . . . ' and he wrote down every single note, in perfect order. That's how the *Miserere* escaped from its locked cabinet. And the son who set it free was Wolfgang Amadeus Mozart.'

Kathy looked at David. 'You have a child genius on your hands,' she said quietly.

He nodded. 'Music is her whole world.'

Sally raced out again: 'I'll play you my most favourite piece of all,' she called back.

'Oh, no,' groaned David, a world of pain

somehow in these two words.

Kathy looked across. 'What's up?' she asked.

He shook his head.

Then the final piece of music came drifting through, another familiar and compelling melody. 'Isn't that the one they always play as a war requiem?' Kathy asked.

'It's Barber's *Adagio*,' Sally replied. 'It isn't supposed to be sad. He wrote it as he watched his own baby rise in his cot and try to stand. Then fall back, and start again. Listen to how he captures that as the music repeats, always getting stronger, and stronger each time, until there's an explosion of joy at the end of it . . . the child has finally managed to stand, holding onto the bars of his cot.'

They listened, and Kathy's vision blurred when the music soared to its triumphant conclusion. 'How could they ever have used that as a requiem? It's so happy!'

'It's a requiem, of sorts,' said Sally. 'That's the Liverpool Philharmonic Orchestra playing . . . if I close my eyes very tightly, and listen really hard, I can still hear my mum playing with them. I can hear her violin, more beautiful than the rest . . . '

She turned to Kathy, silent tears cascading down her cheeks.

'It's not fair,' she said brokenly. 'I can hear my mum in her music . . . I can see her in the photos everywhere . . . but I will never, ever, be able to throw my arms round her again, then hug her tight, and tell her how much I love her . . . '

Instinctively, Kathy opened her arms to the girl.

But it was to her father that she ran, and the silent tears became a storm of weeping. Kathy watched helplessly, seeing the tears of pain roll down David's face, as he held her close.

'Can I help?' she whispered.

He shook his head.

'Should I go?' she asked.

He hesitated for a moment, then nodded, fractionally.

Kathy gathered her coat and tote bag, then stood watching in the doorway of the dining room. Father and child were still in each other's arms, the girl's sobs slowly quietening. Kathy wanted to say something, anything.

But she turned, letting herself silently out of the house.

Feeling, all the time, that she had unwittingly and unwillingly become an intruder in a world of sorrow which still filled this house to overflowing. Father and daughter had only each other, and were all that was left of what had been a very complete and once-happy family.

A family to which Kathy could never belong . . .

⋆ ⋆ ⋆

'That smells good.'

Noel turned from the cooker, to find Henrietta's face at the cabin door.

'Come in,' he said. 'Close that door — it's parky out there.'

'Cold? You're joking! It's a nice spring evening.'

'Wait until you're my age,' he grimaced.

'By then, I'll have forgotten what I'm waiting for . . . '

They grinned at each other, mutual liking strong. Two no-nonsense people.

'A mug of tea?' asked Noel. 'Better still, a glass of wine? I was just about to add some to the pot.'

'Why? What's cooking?' she asked.

'Chilli. An authentic Mexican recipe with hints of Paris, Glasgow and Dundee cuisine added. The wine's from Glasgow . . . '

'I didn't know there was wine in chilli,' Henrietta objected.

'There's wine in everything, after you've been to Glasgow.'

He disappeared forward, then emerged, bottle of Merlot in his hand. 'It's supposed to breathe. But if we pour it into glasses, that leaves a broader surface to do the breathing.'

'If you say so.'

'Trust me, I have a diploma in cooking from a French college. Mind you, it wasn't mine — but I kept it, in case it came in useful. The glasses are behind you.'

'I'm waiting to see how much wine you put into chilli.'

'In creative cooking, both amount and method are optional. You can add wine to taste, when cooking, or sip the wine while you cook, then add meat later — again to taste. The second way's more fun, I always think. Cheers! What brings you here?'

'I was looking for Becky — where is she?'

'Up at the village park. Mike dropped in, to take Jon there to play football. He coaches kids. I was ordered to get supper ready for them coming back.'

'Then I'd better not stay . . . ' She half-rose.

'Have you eaten already?'

'No, but . . . '

'Then we've food a-plenty. If we all cram up, there's room at the table for five — two on each side, one at the open end. So long as we keep our elbows to our sides, when we're eating.'

'That takes away half the fun,' protested Henrietta.

They heard the sound of laughter on the canal bank.

'That's them now,' said Noel.

The *Ella Mae* rocked slightly, as the others stepped aboard. More laughter.

'There was a time, when I thought I'd never hear her laugh again,' he said quietly. 'That's a good sound. So whatever has caused it, is good.'

The cabin door opened, and Jonathon came skipping down the steps.

'Well?' demanded Noel. 'Is he another David Beckham?'

'Not yet!' Jonathon grinned. 'But Mike says I have the makings.'

'And he should know,' Noel said. 'Hi, Mike. Is he going to earn enough to keep his old uncle better than his old uncle ever managed?'

'He did just fine,' said Mike. 'Hi there, Henrietta.'

'Mike.' Gathering her wine glass, she slid up to the end of the bench seat.

'Oh, no. He's done it again,' Becky groaned. 'Where do you get that wine?'

'The fairies keep bringing it,' said Noel.

'And it's bad luck, to turn away a fairy's gift,' said Henrietta.

'I was going to say the very same myself,' smiled Noel. 'Help yourselves — I'm busy here, adding the final touches. Where have you hidden the basmati rice?'

'Where I found it,' Becky said. 'In that cupboard. Hi, Henrietta. No problems, I hope — you haven't discovered another sack of invoices, have you?'

Henrietta turned to Noel. 'When I was her age, I respected the elderly.'

'When I was her age,' said Noel, 'there weren't any elderly. Just a guy called Adam, hiding behind a dustbin from a woman called Eve.'

'No doubt he had good reason,' said Becky. She looked quizzically at Henrietta.

'I'm here for dinner,' she said apologetically. 'Invited by the *chef*.'

'Did nobody warn you about his cooking?'

'It smells good.'

'It's downhill all the way from there.' Becky accepted a glass of wine, handed over by Mike. Their fingers brushed, and she smiled up at him. Henrietta noticed, and thought that she could make a good guess at what was cheering up Becky. Good luck to them both. Mike was a solid lad, his head untouched by all the rubbish written about him in the football press.

'I've come here with a problem, Becky,' she said.

The end of my job, thought Becky, panicking.

'Oh, yes,' she said calmly. 'How can we help?'

'If you can't, I'm in trouble.' Henrietta pushed her glass aside. 'We've two teachers in the village school. Miss Forbes, the head teacher, and Pop Bailey, who has been with us for forty-plus years. He's well into his seventies, but we keep him on. He's the same good teacher he always was. However, it's getting too much for him, and he's asked me to let him retire. If I do, he'll be dead in a couple of months. So I want to keep him working part-time, easing him into retirement — and to do that, I'll need another teacher. But I've no time to advertise, and interview people I don't know or trust. Not for a part-time post.'

The light-blue eyes looked steadily at Becky. 'Cluny's Foundation is my school. I'm the gaffer, and the final shout is mine. I need a part-time teacher I can fire, if things don't work out. Someone I can trust, who won't go whimpering to any court.'

A grim smile flickered. 'This isn't fair — you're already working for me, without a contract. Learning on the job and producing miracles. Are you willing to jump into another deep end? Forgetting all your big-class experience down south, and learning to handle small groups of kids, like we do up here? Three days a week, no contract. And no mercy, if you can't adjust . . . '

6

The silence stretched. Henrietta raised her glass of wine and slowly sipped, her eyes never leaving Becky's.

'I'm waiting,' she said gently.

Becky's mind was spinning. It was one thing to accept a part-time job as office assistant, and be glad of the money — not to mention the excuse to stay on at Longbank for longer than planned. But quite another, to take on a teaching job in a small village school. A job which could turn out to be life-changing, rather than temporary. Henrietta's offer could shape her entire future.

'You scarcely know me,' she said quietly.

'I've seen enough.'

'This is children's education we're dealing with . . . If we get it wrong . . . '

'We won't.'

'I've never taught in mixed-age classes before.'

'You'll learn.'

'We're in the middle of the summer term — with its final pupil assessments to carry out. I'd have to hit the ground running, when I don't know anything about all this strange cultural and society stuff I've heard you talking about.'

'Pop Bailey will handle these. He says that you can take the normal curricula, leave him with the bells and whistles. He can tell you exactly where he's taken the kids, and where they have to be by end of term. So, what's your problem?'

Clearly, Henrietta had talked her idea through, before coming here. Taking on board others' opinions. Good, and typical of the woman. For someone who could be hard as nails, she knew when and how to carry people with her.

Becky sighed. 'I don't see any fairy godmother wings,' she said.

'Where?'

'Behind you.'

That wonderful smile again. 'Wore them out years ago, carrying coal.'

'I can only promise to try my best,' said Becky.

'That's good enough for me.'

'OK,' said Becky. How did they seal a bargain up here? She spat into her hand, and held it out.

'Becky! What on earth are you doing?' exclaimed Noel.

'Keep out of this, it's women's work. And an old local custom.'

134

Henrietta grinned. 'You learn fast.' She spat into her own hand. 'So, it's a deal, then? You give it your best shot. Pop and Miss Forbes will be there to help you. And if it doesn't work out, then you're fired. No comeback, no industrial tribunals. You step aside and I try to find somebody else to take over.'

'Deal,' Becky said quietly.

They shook hands, a firm no-nonsense clasp. The agreement sealed, without writing, by something which mattered more up north. By word of honour.

'I'm starving,' Henrietta said. 'When's he going to serve that chilli?'

★　★　★

Kathy waited, out at the edge of the Ribble Estuary, for the figure of the solitary runner to catch up with her.

'Hi, David,' she said quietly. 'I was hoping you'd be out this morning.'

He nodded. 'Likewise. My heart did a cartwheel, when it saw you out in front of me, waiting.'

They began to run, easily and companionably, side by side.

'I'm so sorry about last night,' Kathy said. 'If I'd known that it was your wife's orchestra playing . . . I'd have thought of something to say to stop her from putting that CD on. My heart was breaking for her — for both of you.'

'She's so quick — it's playing, before I can stop her. And why should I stop her? It's all she has left of her mum, hearing Beth do what she did as naturally as a bird sings. But it always ends in tears, and takes Sally days to get over it. There are times I wonder if she's ever going to let go, and move on with her life.'

David paused, as a squall blasted in from the grey estuary. Amid its noise, he would have had to shout. Once they had run through its disturbance, he glanced over at Kathy.

'At first, I thought it would help,' he said. 'You know, act as a release, a cleansing, for her grief. But she won't let go. Every time it happens, it's as if it's the first time that her mother's loss has hit her.'

'And you . . . '

Running easily, he shrugged. 'You can bury someone, but that never takes them out of your life. There are always memories. Good memories. So I hurt for Sally — and, yes, I hurt for myself.'

'Normal, I would guess,' said Kathy. 'You can't just switch off love.'

'No you can't,' he said bluntly. 'And that

makes it difficult to pick up the threads of your own life again.' He glanced across at Kathy. 'You meet someone you really like and somehow that still feels as if you're cheating on her. That's why I was so slow to answer, when you asked that time. I still hadn't got things sorted out in my mind.'

'But you have, now?'

They ran in silence for a bit. 'I think so,' he said at last. 'It would be easier if Sally didn't keep the kettle boiling, bringing everything back to the surface again. I want to be honest with you. It can still be a problem.'

Kathy stopped and caught his arm.

'Look, I can step aside,' she said quietly. 'Out of your life. Completely.'

'Why? That's the last thing I want. I want to see where this . . . friendship . . . takes us. Maybe lean on you, to help us work this through.'

'I feel outside it all. An onlooker, unable to do the one thing I want to do, which is to help you both. An intruder — the opposite side of what you mentioned a minute ago. Last night I felt as if I was stealing you from your wife, or at least from her shadow. And I hated feeling so cheap.'

He gripped her arms. 'You mustn't feel like that,' he said intensely. 'You are outside this, but in the best possible way. You're beyond

Beth's shadow, you're from a future that we're trying to reach. You've nothing to do with her loss. You are Kathy, a different, later chapter in our book. If we get muddled, or down, it's got nothing to do with you. It's all about Sally and me, still adjusting to Beth's loss.'

Another squall blasted over, soaking them. Neither noticed.

'It's all so difficult,' he said desperately. 'Nobody ever teaches you, or tells you what to do. You're left to blunder through all the pain and grief, and find a way of sticking your daughter and yourself back together again. Like broken Humpty Dumpties. Sometimes mending works — you're both still intact, at the end of the day. But every now and then, like last night, it all comes apart again, and you don't know where to start, or what to do to make life more bearable.'

He must have loved Beth very much, Kathy thought bleakly. They both had, father and daughter. Setting up in their minds an invisible competitor, too perfect in memory ever to be beaten in an honest race. Did she want to get involved in this? Did she have any choice? She was already more serious about this man than any other who had come into her life. In her heart, she knew he ticked all her boxes, was a near-perfect fit for the life's partner she'd been looking for. Only he came with a tangled mess of emotions, for another woman who had once filled his life. If their future was to be linked together, first she must help him — and herself — to come to terms with that past.

'We can only let things flow on, and see what happens,' she said quietly.

'Exactly. Please be patient with me — with us.'

Kathy's heart sank. The daughter. Another woman's daughter, who would likely see her as a predator on her dad.

She shivered: was she crowding onto someone else's grave, or was their shadow reaching out already to touch her? Warn her off?

'Let's run,' she said. 'I'm getting cold.'

★   ★   ★

'Well, I'll leave you to it,' said Henrietta. 'I've a business to run.'

She shot off, leaving Becky standing awkwardly with the two older teachers from the school. It was lunchtime, and the air was full of children's voices: twenty-six healthy kids, running round a playground, make as much noise as a hundred.

'It's good to have your help, Miss

Calderwood.' Miss Forbes was a tall thin lady, prim and tense. Throughout Henrietta's introduction she had smiled and nodded endlessly in an apparent attempt to cover her nerves. This woman was either scared of Henrietta, or in awe of her, Becky thought.

'I can only promise that I'll do my best,' she said.

'Quite. Now, if you'll excuse me, I have work to set up for the children . . . '

They were like ten green bottles standing on a wall, Becky thought wryly, reduced to eight and counting.

'Liza is a wonderful teacher,' Pop Bailey smiled. 'She's not rude — just desperately shy. Put her in front of a crowd of kids, push a stick of chalk into her hand, and she becomes a magician.'

Faded blue eyes twinkled from beneath hugely overgrown eyebrows. He looked like a rubicund character who had wandered benignly in from one of Charles Dickens' novels. Becky decided that she liked this man, on sight.

'I can sympathize,' she said wryly. 'I'm scared too.'

'Fiddlesticks!' He took her by the arm and guided her inside. 'You'll take to this like a duck to water. Knew that, the moment I clapped eyes on you. Come and I'll show you the classroom we'll share. Then I'll take you through the work we're doing, and what you need to prepare. You'll be fine — another Liza Forbes, just wait and see. Henrietta vouched for you.'

'She did?'

'Absolutely. And her judgement of people is never wrong.'

'There's always a first time!'

'Rubbish! Here's my den. I stepped into it fifty-three years ago, as a young man. Now, I'm trying to tunnel out and escape from it, to put my feet up and have a well-earned rest.'

Becky smiled at him. 'Look at me in the eye, and tell me that you really want to leave,' she challenged.

Pop snorted with laughter. 'Is it that obvious?'

'To another teacher. Teaching is your life.'

'And Burnley Football Club.'

Becky laughed. 'It takes all kinds, I suppose.'

'Even Clarets-mad fans. Now, here are the current projects . . . ' and Pop launched into a description of what he'd been trying to bring from the curriculum into learning-by-doing projects, the problems that had emerged, how he'd tackled them, where the pupils should go next. Becky felt overwhelming relief: whatever the school's odd culture, this was no different from how she would have tackled it herself.

Forty minutes passed, two teachers engrossed in their craft, the air buzzing with questions and answers.

'You'll do fine,' promised Pop. 'And you won't be on your own, Liza and myself will keep an eye on you . . . ' He glanced at his watch. 'Better eat my sandwiches,' he apologized. 'Else I'll be spraying crumbs over the class.'

'Thanks, for taking me through this,' Becky said.

'Pleasure. Find your own way out? Head towards the noise.'

'See you on Wednesday morning,' she said.

With all her heart, she wished she could start right now, when her mind was in tune with what the kids were doing. Just getting them to explain how they had got there, and what they had learned, would break the ice — and would be exactly the presentation/analysis approach which was central to modern learning.

She sighed: when you're in the middle of a lions' cage, it's never as scary as the prospect of having to go in there and face the lions. You're too busy thinking on your feet, to be afraid. Watching faces, searching kids' eyes for puzzlement or understanding, then either finding a new way to explain the material, or moving on.

Becky pushed through the swing doors, into the spring sunshine. For a moment she stood on the steps, smiling at how the kids had split up to do their different things. Girls with their skipping ropes — the ancient toy which had survived the electronic revolution. Boys and their endless football matches.

'Over here, Jonno!' A shrill voice, full of urgency.

The ball must have come to him, because all the opponents converged, apart from one small figure who sprinted forward, in anticipation of the return pass which split the defenders' ranks. The small figure pounced on the ball, and scored between the goalposts of piled-up jackets and jerseys.

'Oh, well done, Jonno!'

Team mates ran to slap the scorer's back, ruffle his hair. The boy looked up, his face radiant as if he had scored a winning goal in front of packed terracing. It was Jonathon.

The scene blurred before Becky's eyes.

God bless you, Mike, she thought. In three short coaching sessions, he had found a way to solve a problem which had defeated her, setting her son's shy steps onto the path towards winning acceptance from his peers. And, already, his football nickname — something he might carry for the rest of his life.

The school bell rang, and the children

broke up, to stand in lines outside the door. Becky watched from the edge of the small schoolyard. She saw Miss Forbes come out, Pop Bailey behind her, his round red cheeks still suspiciously full and chewing. She sensed the mutual trust and liking between children and their teachers. A small, secure world. Saw the shy Liza Forbes in a new role, as the calm and confident head teacher in front of her pupils.

Becky stood until the last child filed into the old school.

Was this what she'd been made for? To live her life away from crowds and fame and fortune? With the only prize in her grasp, the knowledge that she was a respected part of an old continuity? Would she be like Pop, entering this strange school as a young woman, to ultimately hand over her classes in trust to someone else, having spent her whole life teaching generation after generation of children in this place? Watching them move on, to make their own lives?

She looked up to the blue hills of the Dales. Right now, there wasn't anything she'd rather do than take over from where that kindly man had finished.

★   ★   ★

'That's it, keep together!' Kathy shouted, above the noise of singing children's voices. She beat time with her right hand as the CD backing track reached its conclusion, then applauded the performers.

'Bravo!' she said. 'Everybody finished at the same time. Nobody came limping in five minutes late . . . which is a change, for some of us.'

'C'mon, Kathy, I was only two bars behind that one time,' protested Jim.

'OK, so you've learned to listen to the others — and sing faster.'

'He's still out of tune,' complained Samantha.

'Look, Sam, for Jim that's as close to tune as he's likely to get.'

'He should have been the family dog.'

'I'm the family dog. I was the first to volunteer.'

'At least you bark in tune . . . '

Flushed faces, sparkling eyes. A contrast to the glum foot-dragging she remembered from rehearsals last year, Kathy thought. This lot were turning into real troupers, as tight-knit and full of banter as a football team,

'We'll kill them when we do this show in two weeks' time,' Jim declared proudly. 'They'll be asking us to sing an encore.'

'Asking us, maybe. Not you.'

'Who says?'

'Let's do that ensemble number again,' Kathy said hastily. 'This time, Donald, don't sing quite so loudly. And Sally, let's hear you a little more. Keep focused, Jim, you're doing fine — just remember it's a chorus, not a solo. And Nigel, pause a fraction before that final set of barks — create tension, that's why the music stops. Ready, everybody?'

Kathy returned to the CD player, skipping to the final track. She pressed play, and let the opening bars blast through. 'Right . . . one . . . two . . . three . . . '

Children's voices filled the classroom — not perfect, but with happy freshness and enthusiasm to spare. It was only meant to be children singing, not a polished choir, she reminded herself. Don't get them too note-perfect. Let them all stay in character, keep their parents smiling.

At last, the rehearsal was over. Kathy cut across the babble of voices, to remind everyone when the next rehearsal would be. Then sagged back wearily, as the kids were collected in twos and threes by the usual long-suffering parents' carpool taxi service.

She was left, as often happened, with Sally, because David always collected them, and took her home. Then came in for a coffee and a chat, while Sally explored Kathy's wide collection of jazz, folk and pop music.

'You did a lot better tonight, Sally,' she said quietly. 'I told you that the words would come to you once you were acting your part.'

'I'm still scared.'

'Why be scared? It's a great show. You're doing just fine — everybody is.'

'I just am. Don't want to be an actor.'

The little girl looked miserable. Kathy gently took her arm.

It was snatched away.

'Want to leave the show,' said Sally. 'Don't want to sing.'

'You have a lovely voice! You sang your duet and your solo great tonight.'

'Don't want to do it. I'm asking Dad to let me leave.'

'You can't leave!' exclaimed Kathy. 'Not now. Not within two weeks of the show. We couldn't train another singer, not in that time. And there's no need for you to leave . . . you've grown into the part quite beautifully. You're a star.'

Sally started crying, silent tears pouring down her face. Was it stage fright, or something else, rooted in her mother's death?

'Oh Sally, please don't cry,' Kathy said gently. She hesitated, then tried to gather the little girl into her arms.

Instant resistance. Two small hands pushed

her violently away.

'Don't do that!' Sally screamed. 'You're not my mum! You never will be!'

'Easy!' said Kathy. 'Calm down. I was only trying to comfort you, show you that I was on your side.'

'You're not!'

'Of course I am . . . '

'It's all an act!' stormed Sally. 'You're trying to show my dad that you care for me. But you don't, not really. You're trying to steal him . . . I saw him holding your hand, the other night. It's not fair! My mum's not here, to look after me and him . . . just let him be, leave us both alone. Go away! I hate you . . . I HATE YOU!'

Stricken, Kathy stared at the girl, searching for words, when there was nothing she could say. Gradually, she became aware of another figure, standing silently at the classroom door. David.

Sally ran to her father, throwing herself into his arms.

Kathy waited, with the same strange feeling as she had experienced after that meal in David's flat. A feeling that she was on the outside, always. An intruder who was trying to worm her way into a family who didn't want her.

Didn't need her, now or ever.

Briefly, over the girl's head, their eyes met. She saw the mute and desperate appeal in his. Then David picked up his daughter and carried her out to the car. The classroom door swung closed, behind him. A pause, then the sound of a car starting up, drawing away. Leaving her standing there.

Something tickled Kathy's cheek. Absently, she lifted her hand, and brushed it away. Then glanced down at her fingers. They were wet, with tears.

Another battle lost, she thought. And, did she really want to fight this war?

★   ★   ★

Mike was waiting for her at the Foulridge bus stop. As she stepped from the bus, he gathered her into a quiet and gentle hug. Becky waited for her ribs to crack, but that didn't happen. If it had, she wouldn't have cared.

'This is really bad,' she said. 'I vowed that, at all times, I would stand on my own two feet. And look at me . . .'

Grey eyes twinkled. 'Well, I've put you down and you're standing.'

'I'm not,' she sighed. 'I feel like a boxer, hanging on for dear life.'

His arm slipped round her shoulders, and she felt herself being steered down to the canal. 'What's a-do, then?' he asked her. 'What's the problem?'

'I just need to hang on to you for a bit. Borrow some of your strength.'

'Feel free. But let me get the kettle going, first. Have you eaten?'

'No. I left Noel to drum up a meal for himself and Jon. And Henrietta's taken to dropping in at supper-time. She must like his cooking.'

Mike grinned. 'I thought it was the way to a man's heart, through his stomach. Not a woman's.'

Becky laughed. 'Nothing like that,' she said. 'They're just good friends.'

'Of course,' he said solemnly. 'Then I'll do a Noel — impress you with my cooking. You've tasted nowt like a Yorkshire trout.'

'From the canal?'

He laughed. 'No way — wouldn't last five minutes in the canal. No, I caught them in a moorland tarn last night. I was going to do them in a salad.'

'I can make the salad,' she said. 'It will take my mind off it.'

They had reached his office, and his flat above that.

'Take your mind off what?' he asked.

'Just scared.' Becky sighed. 'I start teaching tomorrow.'

'OK, so you're a teacher. Maybe a bit short of match practice, but still a teacher. You'll be fine, once you get going.'

'Everybody says that!' Becky blurted out. 'But this is a different kind of teaching. The only teaching I know is with single-age classes — everybody at the same stage, some quicker, some slower, than the rest. In the Cluny Foundation, there are only two classes. Ages five to fourteen, spread between them. Kids at different levels, learning different things — how do you give a lesson? What do you talk about? How do you prepare for everybody?'

Mike ambled over to his fridge and brought out a plate with four gutted trout lying across it. He turned on his cold tap, and began to rinse the fish.

'Sounds just like coaching,' he finally said.

'What does?'

'Different ages, different levels. Every coaching session of kids is like that.' He began to search through his cupboards. 'Ever tasted a trout rolled in oatmeal?' he asked over his shoulder. 'It means frying them, but it brings out the flavour.'

Becky sat on the edge of the kitchen table.

'So, how do you handle it in a coaching session?' she asked, frowning.

'Only way you can. Talk to them for a bit

about something general, then get them all working on their own thing. Let them work, while you go round them . . . a bit of praise here, change what they're doing somewhere else, keep encouraging them to do it better, quicker. Keep 'em all working hard at whatever it is they're doing. Then bring them together at session's end, and set them a general exercise, where they can all chip in and show what they've learned.'

He turned, frying pan in hand. 'It's the best way to teach. You're working with individuals, or small groups. Going from one to t'other. Giving each kid exactly what they need in skill, or confidence, keeping everybody on their toes. And staying on your own front foot, without even trying. Brings out the best in you.'

'That helps,' she said thoughtfully. 'But all the different ages . . . '

'They won't all be different ages,' he said reasonably. 'You'll have maybe three, at worst four groups, with two or three kids in each. Get each group pulling together, helping each other. Works a treat in football.'

Becky laughed. 'But maybe not in the rest of the world.'

Mike grinned. 'Oh, you'd be surprised,' he said. 'I teach football as a way of learning to work as a team. Of finding out their strengths and using them, or knowing where they're weak, and covering for them. Of getting beaten, and picking themselves up again. Of winning, and learning not to crow too loud — because there's always somebody better. Kids will find a lot of these skills useful in their lives. Long after they quit playing football.'

'Mike,' she sighed. 'You're a philosopher.'

He looked at her ruefully. 'A better philosopher than a cook.'

'Sit down,' ordered Becky. 'Give me these trout.'

He watched her work, smiling. This was the woman he had searched for, all his life, he thought. Bright and brave, easy on the eye and on the ear. He liked her humour, and her sudden serious moods. Liked the way she leaned on him — and he, increasingly, on her. He liked the way things were going but, as with the canal, it was better to let what happened flow at its own natural pace.

A memory stirred, less than half-formed, in his mind.

'There was a guy I heard about at school,' he mused. 'A poet.'

'Uhuh. And?'

'And ... something he said ... about being in a desert — or was it an oasis?' Mike found himself turning red, and prayed that

Becky was too busy to notice. He had just remembered the full quotation, and knew that it led to deep waters.

'Right,' she said, 'he was in a desert or an oasis. He probably knew which was which, even if you don't. He was a poet, a man of words, so what did he say?'

'I've forgotten,' Mike evaded. 'Something about wine.'

'You're as bad as Noel,' Becky complained. Then, suddenly, she knew. The hair on her neck prickled. 'Omar Khayyam,' she whispered. 'It was him, wasn't it?'

'Could be.'

' . . . a glass of wine, a loaf of bread, and thou beside me in the wilderness,' she quoted softly. 'Then that wilderness, is paradise enow.'

'Something like that,' he muttered. 'Give or take a bit.'

'You thought of that?'

'I did. And I've thought of something else as well.'

'Which is?'

'I've a loaf of bread in the larder. And I can nip to the Costcutter and get a bottle of white wine . . . and . . . '

Becky came over, and carefully placed her oatmeal-covered hands behind his head. Such a huge strong neck, for a quiet man, she thought. Her gentle giant.

'Mike,' she said. 'I don't need the wine, and I don't need the bread just yet . . . I've got all I need right here.'

He looked down into her face, knowing deep in his heart that he loved this woman and that, as time passed, he would only learn to love her more.

'All you need? And what's that?' he asked.

'You,' said Becky.

* * *

Becky pushed through the school doors, her heart hammering, almost climbing out of her chest and into her throat. Inside, she found Pop Bailey leaning nonchalantly against the corridor wall, and studying a well-used piece of chalk in his fingers.

'What are you doing here?' she demanded. 'This is supposed to be your day off, from now on.'

The eyebrows bristled like an ancient and overgrown hedge.

'I'm old,' he said mildly. 'I forget things. I forgot it was my day off.'

'Liar, liar, pants on fire.' She found herself smiling.

He pushed himself away from the wall, and craned stiffly round. 'Not yet,' he said. Then the blue eyes twinkled up. 'Solidarity. We're in the same life's calling, so I came to wish you well. To walk you down the corridor, in case you've forgotten where my classroom is.'

'Hey!' she protested. 'I'm not that old.'

Pop grinned. 'You will be, one day.' He fell into step alongside her. 'About a hundred years ago, a batty old lady walked me down this selfsame corridor, when I was every bit as scared as you. She smelled of mothballs in the wardrobe, but I've spared you that. She talked to me, and calmed me down. She told me that I would be just fine — and look at me now. I have my own sorcerer's apprentice and the only fear I've got is that, one day, it will all be over, and there will be nothing left for me to do.'

'Not for many, many years,' said Becky.

'Old teachers don't die, their chalk-marks simply fade away,' Pop smiled. 'Look at me, Becky Calderwood. One day, a hundred years from now, this will be you.'

Becky's eyes filled. 'Are the eyebrows optional?' she asked.

Pop grinned. 'You can always hire a pair.'

She reached out, and hugged him. 'I'll borrow yours,' she whispered.

They stood, outside the classroom door. Inside, the electric hum of children waiting. Becky gulped, and reached for the ancient wooden doorknob.

'Hang on,' said Pop. 'You've forgotten something.'

'What?' she asked, throat so tight, she could barely speak.

'This.'

He held out his stick of chalk to her.

'It's the nearest thing I could find to a baton, to pass on,' he smiled.

'Will I be worthy of it?'

'I'll eat it, if you're not. Good luck, lass.' He turned away.

'Thank you,' she said. 'Pop . . . I don't even know your real name.'

'I've been Pop so long, I've almost forgotten. Clarence. Wouldn't you rather be called Pop?' His smile was more than a smile: there was a lifetime of understanding in it, a wisdom which came from many years of turning children into adults, of watching the world like an ancient soul who had come back to help.

'Go for it,' he said. 'You were born and made to teach here. Trust me.'

Becky looked down at the well-worn chalk stick in her hand.

'I'll try to live up to this,' she whispered.

Then paused, and took a deep, shuddering breath. Her whole future, hers and Jon's, depended on this. Doing this work, living in this small town at the foot of the Dales, a future — maybe — with Mike at her side. They all trusted her, Noel, Mike, Henrietta, and now Pop. Could she make the change, to teaching small, fragmented rural classes? Could she earn their trust?

Becky swallowed, steeled herself, and opened the classroom door.

7

Noel looked up from his book. 'Well, how did you get on?' he asked.

Becky slumped wearily onto her seat. 'The day went so quickly, and I was so busy setting up work for the kids to do in the afternoon, that I forgot my lunch,' she said. 'I never had time to be scared. Now that it's over, my legs barely carried me home.'

Noel closed his book. 'These sandwiches,' he said, 'get them eaten now. I'll make us both a pot of tea.'

'I'm too tired to argue.' Becky rummaged in her bag and brought out dry and crooked sandwiches. She took a reluctant bite, then stared in surprise to find the sandwich gone and her fingers reaching for another. 'They've kept well,' she said indistinctly.

'Let me make you fresh . . . ' Noel started.

'Too late.' Becky dusted her hands. 'Where's that mug of tea?'

'Is teaching going to make you bossy?' Noel demanded, bringing it over.

'No. I was bossy before I started teaching. Somebody has to organize people . . . ' Becky drained the mug. 'I'm as bad as Henrietta,' she sighed. 'Lord knows what I'd be like if I was carrying coal.'

'Covered in black dust, rather than chalk dust,' Noel said.

'I'm not, am I?'

'Unless it's dandruff.'

Becky coughed. 'I've never stopped talking all day . . . what with four groups of kids, all asking questions. My voice is ruined.' She kicked off her shoes. 'Ah . . . that's better. It's a while since I've been standing so much.' She gulped through her second mug of tea. 'Noel,' she said. 'I don't suppose the fairies have been at it again, have they? Leaving the odd bottle of Merlot through in your cabin?'

Noel considered. 'Not recently.'

'Damn,' said Becky. 'I wanted to celebrate.'

'Where's Jon?' he asked.

'Stayed on at school — to play football.'

Noel nodded. 'So Mike was right, a little coaching worked the trick.' He paused. 'Were you serious about that wine?'

'Not serious enough to go back up the village, and buy a bottle.'

'No need,' said Noel. 'There's white wine chilling int' fridge — as they say oop here. I thought your throat might need some cooling down.'

'Noel,' she said. 'You're an angel.'

'I know,' he said modestly. 'Small glasses, or large ones?'

'Need you ask?'

'Right, hip-bath size.' Noel rummaged through the cupboard.

'Make that three . . .' The *Ella Mae* rocked slightly, as Henrietta came down the cabin steps.

'Oh,' said Noel. 'Do come in. A mug of tea?'

She shook her fist at him.

'All right,' he sighed. 'But we've only got two big glasses.'

'No problem. Look out a small one, for yourself.'

Noel grinned. 'Before you ask, she did fine. A bravura performance.'

Henrietta cocked an enquiring head in Becky's direction.

'I survived,' said Becky. 'At least I didn't make any mistakes that I can remember now. The kids were great — full of enthusiasm. And Miss Forbes told me to call her Liza, in the afternoon.'

'She's never told me that!' Henrietta exclaimed.

'She's scared of you.'

'Me? Never!'

'You can be a very scary person — especially with paperwork.'

Henrietta raised her glass. 'To our stroppy new teacher,' she toasted.

Noel shook his head. 'You're supposed to propose a toast with a full glass,' he objected. 'Not one that's already half empty.'

'Oh,' said Henrietta, crestfallen. 'Well, we can soon put that right.' She held out her glass to Noel. 'Fill this up and I'll propose the toast again — only, this time, I'll do it properly . . .'

★ ★ ★

Out on the road beyond the promenade, the sun was oppressively warm. For once, there was no wind blowing from the estuary; yet, paradoxically, Kathy was finding it harder to run through the motionless air than against a gale.

Her heart wasn't in it. She slogged on, heavy-legged. This was the fourth day she'd been out, and David wasn't there.

A stream of tourist cars, heading to Southport, crowded her into the side of the road and left her choking in their dust. Kathy stopped, hands on knees, her chest heaving as she tried to catch her breath.

Out over the marshland of the Mere, she heard the bubbling call of a curlew — normally one of her most favourite sounds. Today, it seemed lost and mournful, doom-laden. Kathy started to run again, stumbled. It was as if her legs were sulking, refusing to listen or obey.

She began to walk, instead of run.

She had never felt so down, so miserable. Normally, after any knock, she bounced back quickly. This time, all she wanted to do was to stay in her flat, pull the curtains closed, and hide in the darkness.

Kathy forced herself into a trot, then a proper stride — but could find no running rhythm. She slowed down again, panting, ultimately dropping back into a slow walk.

This was no good. The problem was in her head — and her heart — rather than her legs. Kathy hesitated, then stepped through the fence boundary into the Mere, walking over to a low mound in the grass. She sat down, the sun warm on her arms and bare legs, staring out over the dark-green rushes and the patches of blue water. A bee buzzed round her, then away. The curlew call came again, more desolate than ever.

This had never happened to her before; the sure and certain knowledge that here was the man she'd been looking for, a soulmate who would share her life, her laughter, and maybe even her tears. This was no casual attraction. At some deep, emotional level, she was already locked into this relationship, however early in its development.

Why was there such a shadow over it? A cold, dark shadow which blighted everything it touched?

David was being torn apart: not just by his old love for his dead wife, but by his living love for his daughter. While Sally was still devastated by the loss of a woman whom Kathy would never know, lashing out against the only target she could find, the new woman in her father's life. Blocking instinctively any movement that her father might make towards someone else — other than her dead mother.

How could Kathy unravel this desolate emotional tangle? Could she lead the father out to love and freedom, while the daughter was clawing him back so savagely? How might she defuse Sally's instinctive hostility and anger?

David had asked her to wait, be patient. But she could wait for months, perhaps years, stranded always on the outside. Waiting wasn't the answer, and Kathy had never been engineered to wait.

There had to be something positive she could do . . . but what?

Kathy's heart ached, until she thought it would physically break, the pain was so great. Her dark head bowed forward, resting on her arms. Tears fell on the sandy ground beneath her legs, disappearing instantly, leaving only a series of small dark hollows in the sand.

This was as close as she had come in her life to utter, abject defeat.

The curlew's call burbled again, from the far edge of the marshes. She scrubbed her face with the back of a sandy hand, and pushed herself heavily back onto her feet. She had stepped back through the boundary wires, before she even checked the busy road. Luckily, it was quiet.

Kathy looked along the training route she normally covered effortlessly; she didn't have the heart to face it today. She would turn for home, she thought, as a solitary seagull glided across her field of vision, followed by another, and another, circling above her. In any tourist area, people meant food. And nobody learned this quicker than your average seagull. They circled hopefully, as she stood with her hands on her hips, watching.

This must be how it felt, to see the vultures gathering round you in a desert, she thought bleakly. When the only way to chase them was to fight back. The image triggered a thought in her brain, which triggered yet another thought.

The slack runner's body suddenly straightened. Kathy's head came up. She moved quickly and easily into her running stride, heading for home. No leaden legs this time: the ground flew beneath her feet. She wanted to get back into town just as fast as she could make it, before she started doubting the idea which had come to her, and slid back into waiting and lethargy.

Kathy was made for action. This was war, for the man she loved and for his daughter's mind. To banish the shadow which was threatening to blight her life, she must fight back. Must somehow give her invisible opponent substance, learn everything she could about her. With knowledge, comes power . . . and she knew where to find that knowledge.

★ ★ ★

'Becky?'

'Hmmm?' Becky looked up from a pile of schoolwork.

'That's Mike walking along the towpath. He's wearing a hollow in it.' Noel's eyes twinkled, but his face was deadpan.

'Is he?' Becky glanced at Jonathon, who was working on the other side of the cabin table. She saw him half-rise, stare eagerly out through the cabin windows, and wave — even if Mike would never see him.

'We're wearing that kettle out,' sighed Noel.

'No time,' said Becky, returning to her work.

Noel stared at her, then went to open the cabin doors as Mike stepped aboard. 'Hi, Mike,' he said. 'What brings you here?'

'Passing through,' Mike said. 'Been working in Skipton, and dropped in on my way home. Hi, Jon — how's that step-over going?'

'Haven't tried it yet.'

'One day you'll do it — without even thinking,' Mike said. He ducked through the cabin door, and came stiffly down the steps, holding all his descending weight on his good knee while the bad one found the step below. It was his one concession to the injury. 'Hi, Becky. Haven't seen you in days. Have you been busy?'

She nodded towards the pile of exercise books. 'You've no idea how much correction there's to do, or how much new ground we cover every day . . . It's like preparing for four classes, instead of one.'

He pulled a face. 'My exercise books were more red ink than black.'

'I doubt that,' Noel smiled.

'It's true. When I was a kid, I used to sit in class with a football between my boots. My teacher always said that if I had my brain in my feet, I would have been a genius.'

'I've got one of these as well,' Becky sighed. 'What have you done to my son, Mike Preston? He's turned into a football obsessive

— I have to tie him to his chair, for homework. What chance have I got with other kids, if my own son never gets his homework in on time?'

'Not true!' said Jonathon, indignantly.

'No football tonight, until you've finished schoolwork — and don't scribble faster, that's not the answer either.'

Mike grinned. 'Glad my mother wasn't a teacher,' he said wryly.

It drew a conspiratorial smile from Jonathon. 'She's OK,' he said. 'Mostly.'

'Thanks,' said Becky. She smiled at Mike. 'Well, are we feeding you again tonight?'

'Fair's fair — you ate my trout.'

'You might have caught other ones.'

'Too busy. The season's picking up. Everybody wants their boats serviced, as of yesterday.' Mike shook his head. 'Why can't they bring them to me over the winter, when they're not being used?'

'What about that cup of tea?' Noel asked patiently.

Mike tilted his head enquiringly at Becky.

'I'm honestly run off my feet,' she said.

'That's my homework done,' said Jonathon. 'Can we kick a ball about?'

'Half an hour,' said Mike. 'I have to get back myself — a rush job to do for tomorrow. But if your mum says your homework is OK, then I can kick a ball about with you for a bit.'

Becky sighed at the hastily scrawled work. 'Oh, go on. We can tidy up that mess, after supper. Mike, you're staying for the meal . . . I'll start cooking, once I finish these.' She was deep in her correction work by the time the two of them had reached the towpath.

'Word of advice, which you're free to ignore,' Noel said quietly.

'Uhuh?' Becky wrote a comment in the margin of a book.

Silence. A silence which ultimately brought up her head.

'All work and no play isn't good,' said Noel.

'But I have mountains of preparation to do after this . . . '

'I know,' he said. 'Been there, done that. And discovered too late that there's a cost involved — a price that you might not want to pay.'

'Cost? Price?' Becky slowly resurfaced.

'Everything you do carries a cost — which is what else you might have done, with the same time. Making space for people who are important to you. When you look back, you see how often you got it wrong and you wish with all your heart that you had done it differently. By then, it's too late . . . '

He was talking about Ella, Becky knew.

'Good times don't last forever,' Noel said gently. 'They stop, without any warning. Then you've all the time in the world for work, because there's nothing else for you to do. That lad out there is run off his feet, but he took time off, to come and see you. When he gets home, he'll be working until long after midnight, to catch up. So can you.'

Becky coloured.

'Go on,' said Noel. 'You can overtake them before they reach the park. I'll do the supper early, and let you both get back to work.'

Becky hesitated, glancing at the pile of exercise books. Then she stood up and swept them together. 'Noel . . . ' she said.

'I know. I'm an angel.'

'No. What I was going to say was more along the lines of nosey, interfering old whatsits . . . '

'Same thing,' he said, complacently.

* * *

The chair on which Kathy was sitting wasn't made for comfort. She shuffled unhappily, flicking through the newspaper articles and glossy still photos spread in front of her. She had searched systematically through the archive boxes for an hour. It was cold — and a little bit creepy — under the Philharmonic Hall. Total silence, whereas the rest of the huge building was full of music from rehearsals, classes, and the noise of school groups touring. Down here, there was nothing but dead history, and herself.

Kathy wriggled on the wooden seat. She had come here, driven by emotion and instinct, feeling that she must find out anything she could about the woman whose shadow kept falling over everything. But this was awful: she felt like a burglar, prowling through someone's empty house. A thief, looking for something, anything, to steal. She shivered, leafing through the reports again.

She had no idea that the Liverpool Philharmonic Orchestra were such regular travellers, performing routinely all over Britain, and to high praise. The press cuttings were full of reports of tours, of virtuosi who were performing with the orchestra, and of concerts played to a standing ovation.

Not a word about her shadow, in any of them.

In stark contrast to the photographs. She picked up one of the orchestra, in jeans and T-shirts, unloading their instruments from a bus and parked truck. As if drawn by magnets, her eyes found the long blonde hair and slim figure among the rest, violin case tucked under one arm, her head thrown back in laughter at something one of the other players had said. The whole group interacting with the comfortable body language of an extended family.

Behind her, the archive door creaked open, bringing the distant hubbub of the different rehearsals and classes, which had been this blonde woman's life.

'Found what you were looking for?' It was the curator, who had studied her for a few long minutes, before taking her down to the basement archive.

'Yes, thanks,' Kathy said.

The man ambled over. 'Which one . . . ah, she was nice. A real lady, always spoke to you, always a smile. Shame, wasn't it? Such a tragedy for her family. The best ones go first . . .'

Kathy nodded, dumbly.

'Ah, well,' he said. 'Just dropped in to check. People can find it a bit weird, stuck on their own down here. Wanted to check you were still alive and kicking.'

'I'm fine, thanks,' said Kathy. 'Won't be long, now.'

The door closed again, snuffing out the sound of a conductor's raised voice reminding the orchestra how to play a complex passage from a symphony.

Kathy laid aside that photo, picked up another. The string section, relaxing in a break between rehearsals. Arms round each other, smiles for the camera from some, a tongue poked out to ruin the informal shot, from a man in a T-shirt. And Sally's mother caught in the act of cuffing him for his impudence.

There were other, more formal photographs, still and cold: the orchestra dressed to perform, and looking as if it simply wanted to get away and get on with the job it was paid to do. The same faces, but without the smiles, their owners withdrawn behind professional masks of concentration.

Worst of all, the photo she had hidden beneath the others — stuffed hastily away as soon as her eyes saw it. Kathy took a long deep breath, then reached slowly to the bottom of the pile, drawing it out again.

A beautiful, posed, yet natural portrait. A tall slim woman, blonde hair sweeping over bare shoulders and her dark performer's evening dress: a quiet and intelligent face, looking directly at and smiling into the camera. A shining violin and its bow held easily in her right hand, while her left hand rested gently on the shoulder of a little girl, who had been dressed specially for the occasion.

Sally, smiling up at her mother, with almost

tangible love and pride.

Kathy's vision blurred. The woman's eyes seemed to leap straight out through the camera to her. No challenge in them. If anything, a quiet and confident assessment, recognition and, ultimately, acceptance.

Kathy turned the photo over, then repacked everything into the different boxes. She had discovered what she could about her shadow, and was now more confused and helpless than before. Through that final photograph she had somehow touched the mind of the woman who stood between the future and herself, to find no silent threat.

Instead, she had found someone with whom she would have been happy, under different circumstances, to have become a friend.

⋆　⋆　⋆

Noel sighed, stretching out long legs from his folding chair. The weekend sun was warm on him, and the towpath round under Skipton Castle thronged with visitors. Sipping lazily from his glass of wine, he watched the world pass by.

'All I need,' he said, 'is a dusky maiden, fanning me with a palm frond.'

Henrietta glanced across from her own

seat. 'Will I go and smear some coal dust on?' she asked.

Noel considered. 'Not quite what I had in mind,' he said.

'Then wave your own palm frond,' she told him.

They sat in companionable silence, until Noel shaded his eyes, peering forward. 'Is that them coming back from the market?' he asked. They were just like any other family group, he thought. A tall man, with a barely noticeable limp, his hands full of plastic bags, a woman carrying her own share and laughing up at him, while a child clutched a single bag and darted round their feet.

'It's good, to see her happy again,' he murmured.

Henrietta smiled. 'You love her, don't you? Her and the boy?'

'No comment.'

Henrietta took a bigger mouthful of wine than she'd intended. Her father and herself had been a family unit, which needed no others, ever. Now he was gone. At times like this, she felt very much alone. She put down her glass of wine, and wiped her nose.

'Hey, wee coal-wumman,' Noel said gently in broadest Scots.

'What?' She blinked away tears.

'You're part of this family, like it or lump it.

You and your coal have crept in here, when nobody was looking. You are welcome, but your coal's rubbish.'

Henrietta stared at him. 'How did you know what I was thinking?'

'I'm a journalist — trained to read other people's minds, when they won't give me a decent quote. Mostly, they've been pleasantly surprised at the quality of their thoughts, when they saw my copy.'

'Maybe. But there's nothing wrong with my coal,' she said.

The boat rocked as the others came on board.

'He's done it again,' groaned Becky. 'I turn my back on him for a few minutes, and there's another opened bottle of wine on the table.'

'That's how fairies work,' Noel explained. 'You never see them. Just, phut . . . ' he clicked thumb and finger, ' . . . and there you are, another gift from the fairy kingdom lies in front of you.'

'Pity they don't mark coursework,' she said. 'Mike's offering to take us round the Skipton Spur — that's the canal loop round behind the castle.'

'Grab the chance!' said Noel. 'That stretch of the canal is shallow — full of rock shelves. Only permitted skippers are allowed to go the whole way round the spur. What's in your bags?'

'Food,' Becky replied. 'I'm relying on the fairies, to provide refreshments. I've got bread, some baking . . . fantastic sausages with meat and herbs in them . . . '

'And she bought me a pair of football boots,' said Jonathon, flourishing one above his head. 'Can I wear them now, Mum?'

'No,' said Becky. 'You'll damage the deck.'

'There's a good thick carpet, down in the lounge,' offered Noel.

Jonathon disappeared in a blur of light.

'You're spoiling that child,' accused Becky.

'Well, I'm a stand-in granddad. And that's what granddads do — pass on bad habits, and encourage kids to bend the law.'

'You score ten out of ten, on that,' Becky sighed. 'When do you want to cast off, Mike?'

Mike looked at the sun, already sliding down. 'Soonest,' he said. 'The spur takes about an hour. Then four swing bridges and three locks to Longbank — that's another two hours' work.'

Becky stared fixedly at Noel.

He sipped wine. 'Am I in your way?' he asked.

'Unless I take your heels, and tip you overboard.'

Noel sighed, and rose to his feet, glass in

one hand, bottle of wine in the other. 'I think she means yes,' he confided to Henrietta.

'Can we sit on the roof?' Henrietta asked.

'Only if you want to be swept overboard by low branches,' Mike smiled.

'Do we really need to sail round this castle?' Henrietta asked plaintively.

'Let's take the best seats at the cabin windows,' Noel encouraged. 'Leave the servants to their menial work.'

'Keep an eye on Jon,' said Becky. 'Don't let him damage anything with these new boots — that's Mike's fault, he encouraged him.'

Mike leaned forward, pressing the starter button. 'He didn't need much encouragement. And I didn't hear you argue with him either.'

'I was outvoted.'

'That's never stopped you before. Right, you're cabin boy. Cast off.'

'Aye, aye, sir,' she said, edging round the narrow footway and stepping ashore. With practised ease, she cast off the mooring ropes. A gentle nudge out, with her foot, and the slow beat of the engine took over to send them smoothly up the canal, past tourists' clicking cameras. 'Remember to smile,' she called down to Noel.

'I'm smiling, I'm smiling,' came the reply.

They chugged up the cleared part of the loop, the stretch which the thirty-minute boat trips used, and pushed beyond the turning basin into a stretch of canal where sheer rock walls towered up at their right, and the branches of overgrown bushes reached low from the other bank. They passed an ancient stone quay, and headed into what seemed almost virgin jungle.

Mike throttled back, edging slowly forward. There came the gentlest of scrapes as the hull bottom brushed a rock shelf. The propeller's slow turning was kicking up clouds of silt from the bottom. Mike edged to the right, another gentle scrape. A dark underwater ridge surfaced, feet away.

Frowning with concentration, Mike steered the old narrowboat through the passage of clear water. The over-hanging branches came lower and lower, until Becky was crouching over the cabin door, catching each long branch and lifting it over Mike's face.

It brought her very close to him. She saw the grey eyes smile, felt the light kiss on her face. 'Not now,' she said. 'Can't you see, I'm working?'

Another branch, another kiss. Then again.

Finally, neglecting her duty, she was gently whacked on the back of the head by a branch which had crept up on her. 'Ouch!' she said.

Mike lifted it easily over them both. 'Becky Calderwood?' he said.

His grey eyes were suddenly serious.

'Yes,' she said, unable to take her own eyes off them.

'I think I love you,' he said gently.

It should have been so easy, but the words froze on her tongue. She fought to respond — but the words wouldn't come.

He lifted another oncoming branch over both of them.

'In fact,' he said quietly, 'I know I do.'

Tears blurred her eyes. 'Not yet, Mike,' she said huskily. 'I want to, but I can't. Cut me a little more slack. There was so much damage done the time before, so many things that were true when we said them. So many promises we tried to keep and couldn't. Let me find my own way through that mess, and maybe start again, with you . . . '

He kissed the tip of her nose.

'Take as long as you need,' he said. 'I'm not going anywhere.'

★　★　★

David looked up from the drawings he was working on, as the doorbell rang again.

'Coming!' he shouted through.

He opened the door to find a bedraggled Kathy, her hair plastered flat from the rain. 'What on earth . . . ?' he exclaimed.

'I walked,' she said, no expression in her voice or on her face.

Gently, he steered her into the flat. 'Take that wet coat off,' he said. 'I'll get a towel for your hair.'

When he returned, she was still standing, head down, a small cluster of drips on the carpet from her ruined coat. He eased her out of that, threw it onto the coat-stand in the hall. 'Here,' he said. 'Dry your hair.'

She looked up at him. 'I've come, to say goodbye,' she said. In that same voice, without expression. Because, if she allowed expression, then all her control would slip — and that could take her anywhere.

'Why on earth would you want to say goodbye?'

'I've been thinking . . .' Water ran from her hair down her face.

'Oh, come here,' David said crossly. He opened the fresh towel and dried her hair as if it was Sally he was handling. Gently, but no-nonsense firm. 'Now, what's all this goodbye rubbish about?'

'It's for the best. I've only just realized how close you were as a family. No wonder: Beth was a lovely person. You must both have loved her very much . . .'

'That's true, but . . .'

Kathy ploughed on as if she hadn't heard,

as if quoting from a script which had gone round and round inside her head until all other thoughts had been driven out. 'I think you're still in love with her,' she said. 'I don't think you're ready to move on yet. And I don't think Sally is ready to let go of the past, and see another woman step into your life. It might have worked, you and me . . . but not now. I got my timing wrong. I met you too quickly, fell for you before you were ready for that. So I wanted to tell you that I think we should end it now. Before we hurt each other — or Sally — more than either of us could take.'

David threw the wet towel onto the carpet and caught her gently by the shoulders. 'Do you want to say goodbye?' he demanded.

'I'm trying to . . . '

'Do you really want us to step out of each other's lives?'

Kathy's brown eyes filled. Slowly, she shook her head.

'Nor me,' he said intensely. 'Beth was my past. Every fibre in my mind and body tells me that you are my future. Because of Sally, it isn't easy. I can't just step away from the past, and do what I want to do. Not when she's needing help so badly, to come to terms with life.'

He drew her into his study; the light was

still on above the sloping desk and its papers. 'You're soaked through,' he said gently. 'I need to drive you home before you catch a chill. But, Kathy, don't go away. Not ever. Please. I know it's difficult for you, but Sally and I are stranded in the middle of a maze and, somehow, we've got to find our way out of it together. Not just Sally and me — all three of us.'

His fingers tightened on her arms, drawing her closer. 'We have to find a way to bring Sally on board about us,' he said desperately. 'If we don't she might always hate you.'

Kathy shivered. Instinctively, he wrapped his arms around her and they were kissing. At first, with passion, then gently. Kathy felt herself melt into his embrace, that moment stretching forever, bringing more love and tenderness than she had ever known. This man was her future.

The front door opened.

David pushed himself guiltily away from her.

'Daddy? I'm home.' Sally, back from school.

'Through here,' he said, stepping apart.

'That's it,' Kathy said, ever so quietly.

She walked through the door, gathering the sodden coat. Passing Sally in the hallway, she said: 'Don't worry, Sally, I'm going ... '

Then, with her final words directed to David, 'And I won't be back.'

The front door closed quietly behind her.

Puzzled, Sally studied her father's grim face. 'What's Kathy talking about?' she asked.

8

'They've always been out to get us,' Liza Forbes said tiredly. 'Officialdom won't rest until they have closed us down, then merged our pupils with the bigger schools in Skipton.'

Henrietta bristled. 'They've tried that before,' she snapped. 'Fat lot of good it did them.' She picked up the letter notifying the school that it would be inspected by an Ofsted team in four weeks' time. 'Our best defence, as always, is to be so good they can't attack us. Score the highest grade we can get, then turn this into a shield to protect our independence against local politicians and officials . . .'

She snorted, thinking that the grind of local axes was more dangerous than distant Whitehall. 'I take it everything's up to scratch?' she demanded.

'Absolutely! What else? We're exactly where we should be on the curriculum, our project work shows good quality . . . while the continuing support of the children's parents is our best advertisement.' Miss Forbes faltered, then turned brick red, realizing she had forgotten to be shy.

Henrietta never noticed. She glanced at Becky. 'Have you been through an inspection before?'

'Once — but that was years ago.'

'She'll be fine,' Pop said mildly. 'And I'll always be on hand to help out where needed.' His eyes twinkled through bushy eyebrows. 'Think of me as a partner in a wrestling tag-team, waiting outside the ropes.'

'I'd rather not, if you don't mind,' said Henrietta. 'Right, I've a business to run. Any problems, flag 'em up. Likewise, anything you need, just call me in.' She looked wryly at Becky. 'Bet I'm the only school board chairman who has coal dust in their hair . . . '

Then she was off, her sturdy legs carrying her small square figure out of the staffroom and purposefully down the corridor.

Liza smiled weakly. 'Henrietta is a force of nature,' she said. 'Like a hurricane, or a flood. She can flatten anything that local officialdom lines up against her. But not Ofsted and the government. She simply cannot grasp the mountain of paperwork that is waiting for us — the Self Evaluation Forms for the school, arguing the case for our grade and offering evidence for inspectors to test, or outlining how we interact with parents, involving them with school policy. That's my job — no sleep or television for the next three weeks.' She sighed. 'I'll start tonight.'

'Want any help?' Pop asked.

'Not really. I must check the paperwork from our last inspection, see what we can use again. Then download the new forms from the Ofsted website, and update everything.' She smiled tightly. 'Working on my own, I can utter wicked words.' Liza, among her friends, was very human. 'But first, I have to survive today — and that means setting up work for the children coming back from lunch. More rushed eating and drinking as I go — no wonder my tummy has been playing up.' She left, clutching her sandwiches and a thermos flask.

Becky raised an enquiring eyebrow to Pop.

He shrugged. 'Liza worries too much — always has. She's gobbled down her lunch for years, then suffered indigestion. That's been really bad, these last few weeks and I've been telling her to see the doc, in case she's got an ulcer. But she's always too busy to take time off and go.'

Becky reached for another sandwich. 'What's an inspection really like, Pop? You've seen off more inspectors than I've had hot dinners.'

'Starting with the Romans?' he asked, his faded blue eyes twinkling.

'The only time it happened to me was in a

big school with masses of staff and classes to inspect. I was a raw beginner and they left me in peace, which was decent of them. Then I got married, and have only just returned to teaching. In this small school, an inspection is likely to be more close-up and personal.'

Pop rubbed his bald head. 'It used to be simple,' he reflected. 'They came to check where you were in the syllabus. Then to sit and listen to how you taught through your lesson plan, watching how you coped with the kids — you know how something always breaks their concentration. A squirrel runs up a tree outside, somebody asks out for the loo . . . and everybody starts talking. That's when we have to act as sheepdogs and round them up again, get them back on course. That's what they're really watching for, how we cope with the unexpected, keep the lesson flowing.'

He sighed. 'Nowadays, everything is hidden behind a smokescreen of buzzwords, paperwork and education slogans. Usually meaning nothing, and dreamed up by people who never could teach, and went into administration instead. It's all aims, and outputs, and the Lord only knows what else. But when you cut through the smoke and mirrors, they are still looking at the basics which make teaching an art, rather than a formula. Are we breaking the lesson into digestible chunks?

Are we communicating these simply to the kids? Is there a good come-and-go between them and us in a lesson? Do the kids understand what we say?' His round face smiled. 'Leave Liza to the paperwork. Don't try anything fancy in front of the inspectors — just be yourself. Forget they're in the room, and get on with what you do best. That's my advice to you.'

'You make it sound so easy.'

'It is easy,' said Pop.

'And you'll be there, to help out?'

The eyes twinkled under their grey hedgerows. 'If nobody likes the thought of me in wrestler's trunks, then I can be a very large fly, perched high in a corner of the ceiling.'

'Just don't fall down, in the middle of my lesson,' warned Becky.

★ ★ ★

The mobile phone rang as Becky was washing up dishes: she sighed in exasperation, drying her hands. Then glanced at the caller's number, and smiled. 'Hi, Mike,' she said.

'Hi, there.'

A silence followed.

'How are you? What are you doing?' she asked.

'Hanging upside down in a boat, and

covered in oil and dirt.'

'You sound like a bad-tempered bat,' she smiled.

'I feel like a bad-tempered bat. Go on, talk to me.'

'What about?'

'Anything — I just need to hear your voice.'

'Idiot! Have you eaten yet?'

'Not easy, when you're upside down.'

'Unless you're cadging food off us, you starve,' Becky groaned. 'I can throw together a quick meal, if you feel like driving up?'

A pause. 'Tempted — but too busy. It's that time of the year. The only spare time I have is on Saturdays, once all the boats have been collected from me. Sunday midday onwards, either repairs are limping in, or new boats are turning up for their annual service.'

Becky curled up on the bench seat. 'Will you manage to eat before Saturday?' she teased.

'Oh, I'll cobble something together, when I get home.' Mike paused, then said: 'How do you fancy going out somewhere at the weekend?'

'All of us?'

'Just you, me and Jon.'

'That would be nice,' she said. 'Anywhere special?'

'I've something in mind ... ' She could sense his smile.

'Where?'

'A surprise. My treat. Leave your exercise books at home . . . '

'You're a fine one to talk!' Becky exclaimed.

★   ★   ★

The final few rehearsals are always edgy, Kathy told herself. Reflecting stage fright from the players, as the actual performance becomes imminent, when words that had come effortlessly before were forgotten, marks missed on the school stage, and spats erupted between increasingly stressed performers. Her job, as director, was to keep the rehearsal flowing, smooth over mistakes, stroke ruffled feathers, and exude a confidence which she didn't always feel herself.

Not easy, when her heart was down in her boots.

At last the rehearsal was over. She sighed and sagged back wearily into her director's chair. The children watched uneasily.

'That rehearsal was seriously bad?' asked Jim.

'Maybe we should get a new family dog,' muttered Nigel.

At least two of the girls were on the edge of tears.

They were needing her, and she had nothing left to give. The tension among the hard-working group was electric. Kathy fought to raise herself, to find some words that would help.

'Hey, guys,' she said. 'It's normal. We're all thinking far too much about the performance. When it comes, and we're up on stage, then we'll be running on adrenalin and focused so hard that everything will come surging through, word perfect. The first laugh we get from the audience will set the place on fire, and you'll give the performances of your lives — trust me on that.'

A memory flashed, then grew in her mind.

'This happens to every performer,' she said, her voice gradually coming to life, claiming the players' attention. 'It's your body storing up its energies for the night ahead. Leaving you so crammed full you can't think straight and stumble over everything, making mistake after mistake. There was a world-famous opera singer, Jussi Björling in the 1950s, who had such a miserable time during his first rehearsals, that he wanted to walk out on his career before it even started. He was gibbering with nerves, on the night. They put two big stagehands on either side of him, to stop him running away. When his cue came, he couldn't move. The stagehands took him by the scruff of the neck and the slack in his pants, and *threw* him onto the stage. He landed, running, then started singing like an angel.'

Silence with smiles, as the kids envisaged this entrance.

'Who's going to throw me on?' asked Nigel.

'We'll chuck a Bonio onto the stage and you can chase it,' offered Jim.

That was better: in an instant, they were laughing and teasing each other and the awful, brittle feel of tension in the air was gone.

She'd done it, but Kathy was feeling worse than ever. It was the director's job to lift the players — but whose job was it to help the director climb back onto her feet and face life again? She watched numbly, as the kids were collected in ones and twos by their parental taxi service.

Only Sally was left, sitting silently hunched in the furthest corner of the rehearsal room and turning her shoulder against her. Kathy wondered how they were going to get through the next few minutes. When the door finally opened, Sally was up in a shot and out to her father's car.

'Great,' Kathy said, resignedly.

David stepped inside the doorway, and quietly closed it. 'Why did you walk out on us like you did the other night?'

'I thought that was pretty obvious.'

'Not to me, it wasn't.'

'You stepped away, as if you were ashamed to be caught with me in your arms. I simply cannot tell you how bad that made me feel, as if I was something you had to hide. That finished it. I was right, first time — you're not ready to move on with your life yet.'

'That's not true,' he argued angrily. 'You're not making enough allowance for Sally, you're expecting her to be adult in her reactions, when she's not an adult, just a lost and lonely little girl.'

'Aren't we all?' said Kathy.

'She's not sleeping at nights, she's so worried. You're driving her too hard in the school play and this whole new relationship thing between the two of us has been the final straw. She can't cope with all these different pressures. I want to take her out of your production, to protect her.'

'Take her out?' asked Kathy. 'Four days before the performance?'

'She simply hasn't four days more of worry, left inside her.'

'All the kids are scared right now!' Kathy exclaimed. 'The last few days before a performance are always horrible. But that's part of what the kids have to learn — to face down their fears, stay true to the team, trust their training and its endless rehearsals. Sure, they'll get their reward from the applause on the night. But nothing's costless, they have to sweat and earn that applause. No gain without pain — you're a runner, you should know that better than anyone.'

'I'm her father, and want her out,' David said grimly. 'The play's your problem. My responsibility is to Sally. She's had as much as she can suffer . . . '

'You can't take her out of the production,' blazed Kathy. 'We can't possibly replace her at short notice, not when she's playing such a key role.' She took a deep, shuddering breath. 'The show must go on — both on stage, and in life. You can't keep wrapping her up in cotton wool, protecting her. She has to learn to stand on her own two feet, and step out from her mother's shadow. You too!'

David's face went chalk white. 'You're asking us to forget that Beth ever lived,' he said tightly. 'That's neither fair, nor possible.'

The battle had spilled, beyond recovery, from the school play into the problems they must face and solve if they were ever going to have a life together. Kathy's heart stopped racing. Suddenly, she felt icy calm.

'I'm not asking that,' she said quietly. 'I'm just asking that you stop burying yourselves together with her, and live your own two lives. Until you do, there's no room for me — or anybody else — in your hearts. I can't step aside and hide, every time Beth's memory comes up. You would never have asked that of her, so you should never ask it from me. I would rather walk away and finish with us, than ever be left feeling like this again . . . '

The door creaked behind them. They both turned round.

Sally was standing there, watching them quietly.

★　★　★

'Wow!' exclaimed Jonathon. 'Seriously cool!'

They emerged from the under-stand corridors to stand high at the top of a passageway down through the seats. On every side, huge stands towered over them, soaring up to seats perched high beneath the roof. Down below, the football pitch was immaculate and very green.

There were still forty minutes until the game, and the stands were almost empty, despite the steady stream of fans trooping in. Jonathon clutched the match programme that Mike had sneaked down to him, and Becky reached forward to adjust the warm black and white scarf she had bought for him on impulse in the Newcastle club shop at ground level outside.

Mike steered them down to row G of seats, and they eased in past the scatter of people already sitting. 'Keep going, Jon,' he encouraged. 'Those are our seats, on the other side of that man in the duffle coat.'

They sat down, the air already electric with the anticipation that any big match brings. Jonathon stared eagerly around the stands and down to the pitch, where players from both teams were going through muscle warm-up routines in their tracksuits.

'Wow!' he said again. 'Is that Cheick Tiote?'

'That's him,' said Mike. 'Mohawk and all.'

'I thought he'd look bigger.' Jonathon sounded puzzled.

'He's only shorter than me by about this . . . ' and Mike held thumb and forefinger apart to show the difference in height. 'He doesn't seem tall, because you're looking down on him, and from miles away. But see how he's towering over Vurnon Anita there.'

He settled back, his shoulder warm against Becky, who was wrapped up as for exploring the Arctic Circle — under Mike's instructions. He looked down at her, smiling. 'Well, what do you think?' he asked. 'This was my patch, for years.'

'Do you miss it?' she asked.

Mike pulled a face. 'I miss being fit. I miss the rough and tumble of the game — guys kicking lumps out of you, then pulling you to your feet. Or reaching up to be hauled to their feet, after you flatten them. You'd never think it, but there's usually good-humoured banter, among the knocks. I miss the excitement of big games, like today's. But not the brou haha that goes with it — fans hounding you everywhere, newsmen and cameras shadowing your every move, the stupid stories they invent about you, to fill their papers. I hated that, and was always glad to go home to the canal.'

'Because you're only a boatman, at heart,' she smiled.

'That's it — never able to deny the Romany blood in my veins.'

Becky smiled, watching Jonathon open, then begin to devour the match programme. Then her question came blurting out, before she could stop it. 'Why did you never marry, Mike?' she asked.

He shrugged. 'It just worked out like that — by accident, not design.'

Becky waited, watching him gathering his thoughts, to give her as honest an answer as he could manage.

'It's part of the football scene, I guess,' he finally said. 'It's a whole way of life — a golden bubble that you climb into as a big club player. At first, as a kid, you're training night and morning, working on improving your game. Sure, you go out with your mates and strut the stage, and sure, there are always girls around — you're spoiled for choice. The more famous you are, the more people cluster round you and you're carried along, living for the moment and the day.'

He stared down at the pitch. 'Then your final injury happens and you can't believe that you'll never play again. Nor can your mates. These days, I would be whisked over to an American sports clinic and come back as good as new. Not then. It was over, and I had to find a way to leave with dignity.' He glanced across. 'Why did I never marry? Because of what happened when I left. Some of the WAGs — that's players' wives and girlfriends — only want to link their arm through fame by being seen with players, becoming celebrities. Not all, by any means. But I picked a bad 'un: the girl I had decided to settle down with simply disappeared. Next time I saw her, she was on the arm of my best mate.'

He looked ruefully at her. 'Fingers burned, I guess. After that, I was happy just to go back to the life I loved, working on boats. I decided that I was better off on my own — until now.'

Becky nodded. 'I know that feeling,' she said quietly. 'It's so hard, just to relax with someone, to give them trust. Even when you want to . . . '

Mike patted her hand. 'No hurry,' he said. 'Better just to let the whole thing flow — slow and steady, like the canal. It takes its time, but always gets you where you want to go . . . '

The man in the duffle coat pushed across Becky. 'Are you Mike Preston?' he asked. 'Can you autograph this programme for me, then I can give it to my grandson?'

'Sure,' said Mike. 'What's his name? Have you a biro?'

He scribbled a message and handed the programme back.

Another hand came from behind, with another programme. And another. Suddenly, half the stand were crowding round the three of them, pushing roughly in. Becky was jostled, then Jonathon.

'Hey, guys . . . give us some room,' pleaded Mike. 'I need space to move my elbow when I write.' But the buzz of recognition showed signs of turning into a noisy brawl. Mike stood up, drawing Jonathon and Becky protectively behind him, pushing the fans away. 'Ease up, guys, Sure, I'll sign your programmes — just stop shoving my guests around.'

The crush got heavier, until stewards stepped in and began to physically haul people back. One forced his way in to Becky's side to shield her, and glanced over to see who was causing the disturbance.

'Jeez!' he said. 'It's Mike Preston. Hang on.' He hauled out a radio-phone and talked rapidly into it. Then nodded and grinned at Mike. 'Come with us,' he said. 'Your ticket's just been upgraded — to the Directors' Box.'

'Oh, no,' groaned Mike.

'Safety first . . . ' The steward took Becky's arm and waved the crowd of fans aside. 'Haway, lads,' he ordered. 'Make space. Ladies and children here.'

They fought their way up against the flow of fans and down into the under-stand corridor, then were led through a concrete maze into one of the plushest reception bars Becky had ever seen. Two besuited, smiling figures rose and came over to shake Mike's hand and offer him a drink. He refused. One of them took over and guided Mike, Becky and Jon — but not before he had his own match programme signed — up a long flight of carpeted stairs into the open stand and padded leather seats. Becky sat down, and became conscious of a number of turning heads from young women sitting down below and across from her. The WAGs. They glanced at her and Mike: blank looks, their memories clearly didn't go back as far as the fans. Then they turned round to watch their own men.

From that point on, the day grew steadily worse. The pressure for autographs was endless, but better managed in this exalted seating. Then at half-time, Mike was taken down and out onto the pitch, to be cheered and applauded by the fans — some of whom could only have heard of him, rather than seen him play.

When he came back to the box, now emptied because the directors had trooped down to the bar below, she saw the sheen of sweat on his brow. 'Are you all right?' she asked.

He shook his head. 'I hate this,' he replied quietly. 'It's been so long . . . I've grown out of it.'

'Let's quit while we're ahead,' Becky suggested.

He looked across. 'Go home?' he asked.

'Back to your famous canal,' she nodded.

'What about Jon?' Mike asked.

The boy looked longingly at the pitch, then up to Mike, torn between missing the rest of the game and wanting to please his seriously famous coach. A Newcastle legend: the Demba Ba and Alan Shearer of his day.

'OK, OK,' he sighed. 'Let's go.'

'Not again,' groaned Noel. 'When I haven't even started to think about cooking dinner.'

'Whazzat?' Becky looked up blindly from her books.

'Henrietta . . . ' Noel walked to the cabin window. 'Something's wrong.'

'What do you mean?'

'The way she's walking . . . like she's carrying a bag of invisible coal.'

His trained journalistic eye had picked up Henrietta's heavy tread along the towpath, the bowed head and shoulders. 'I'll get the kettle on,' he said. 'You go and meet her — and be prepared for something bad.'

Becky flew from the table and up the steps, surprised at the strength of concern she felt for her friend and employer. She jumped ashore and ran along the towpath.

Henrietta looked utterly defeated, lost and drained of strength.

'What's up?' Becky asked, grasping an arm that felt as if it needed support and, somehow, steering.

Henrietta shook her head, unable to find any words. Becky guided her on board and down the steps, where Noel was pouring a fresh mug of tea. Quietly, eyes sharp, he watched her.

'Out with it,' he said. 'It's better shared, between friends.'

Henrietta sighed, from the soles of her feet.

'Is it the school?' Noel asked.

She nodded.

'Some new crisis?'

Henrietta looked up, eyes brimming. 'The worst thing that could have happened,' she mumbled.

A smile quirked on Noel's lips. 'You could have dropped down dead on us.'

Henrietta blinked. 'Worse than that,' she said.

'There's nowt worse than that,' he told her sternly. 'As long as you're alive, that old school has its champion still in the saddle. And as long as you're in the saddle, then your school has a chance.'

Henrietta sniffed, then looked up at Becky. 'Liza's been taken into hospital,' she said quietly. 'Appendicitis, maybe. The doc fears for peritonitis, from the pain she's in. I'm worried sick. Pop's been telling her for weeks, to go for a check-up. But . . . ' and the tears spilled over, 'what are we going to do about the school inspection? We can't cope with paperwork, or owt, without Liza here to do it for us. Nor the teaching either.'

Becky leaned over the table, her mind racing.

'Pop could come back to teach . . . '

'His back's gone. He's in bed.'

'He'll crawl in, if he's needed,' Becky said. 'I know the man. If he can do even a bit of teaching, I can visit Liza and find out what she wanted to say in the forms, then do it for her. And . . . ' She stood up, smacking a fist into the palm of her other hand. 'And I can maybe get you the best natural teacher I've ever known . . . Kathy, if she'll come. If this works, Henrietta, we're home and dry. I'll complete the Self Evaluation Forms, Pop and Kathy can share Liza's class, and I'll take over my own class, full-time.'

'But the contracts . . . ?'

'This is an emergency!' said Becky. 'We're all mucking in, to save the school. You keep the vultures away from us, and we'll do the rest. We can sort out the contracts later — or not at all. Nobody is going to rock the boat for you.'

Henrietta reached sightlessly for the mug of tea. Drained it in one long swallow, slammed it on the table, and stood up.

'This Kathy of yours,' she said. 'How do we know if she can help?'

'One way to find out,' said Becky, lifting her mobile phone.

★ ★ ★

Even in the far-off rehearsal room, the din of cheering and applause could still be heard. The play had been a real blockbuster — the biggest success in everyone's memory. Which was good. But most satisfying of all, her troupe of performers had played out of their collective skulls, and the songs and dialogue had simply zinged across the audience. The three main songs and two choruses had even been encored, the audience refusing to let the show go on, stamping their feet until Kathy had nodded for a reprise.

Amid the clutter of bags and coats, she paused, then reached into her shoulder bag and found a sheet of paper and a biro. She hesitated, then wrote: *Sally — I told you that you would be our star. At least I got that bit right*. Then, before the impulse died in her, she folded the paper and slipped it into the girl's coat pocket.

The distant din went on: the bittersweet sound of success. Kathy listened, head to one side, then lifted her coat, opened the door, and stepped out. She zigzagged through the parked cars in the playground and walked steadily down the street towards the bus stop. As the local bus slowed down and stopped, she lifted her head towards the sound of a seagull, calling in the dusk above the town. Seagulls never slept — they had one eye open for food at all times, and could spot a discarded takeaway from the other side of town.

Sitting alone in the empty bus, her shoulders slowly rounded and her head drooped. Normally, she would have snapped erect and scolded herself. Tonight, worn out by the strain of rehearsals, and with a heart which felt like lead, she couldn't be bothered. With very little encouragement, tears would flow.

Not that. She wasn't turning into a crybaby. Not for anything, or anybody.

Kathy forced her head up, made herself take an interest in the townscape as it passed. An interest which watched, but didn't really register the blur of neon lights and shopfronts. In fact she missed her stop, and had to walk back in what was now darkness.

Hands deep in pockets, she wandered slowly along the pavement, turning dispiritedly into her street and climbing the steps to her door. Still on automatic pilot, she closed it gently behind herself, a dull headache pulsing above her eyes. It didn't matter. Nothing did, any more. Kathy kicked off her shoes, and threw her bag aside.

Her mobile phone fell out, bouncing across the floor. Listlessly, she picked it up and switched it on. It had been off through the hours of the school performance. While it booted up, she set it on the table-top and went through to the kitchen to pour a glass of wine.

In the distance, her phone buzzed. A delayed text message coming in. It could wait. She wandered back to the living room, glass in hand, and switched on a television set, which she seldom used. Music was her refuge, not the telly, but tonight she felt too down, too raw, to turn music loose on her emotions.

As the set droned out its rolling 24-hour newscast, she reached over to the phone and checked it. From Vodafone: a missed phone call and a voicemail message. Kathy scrolled down to voicemail, dialled and listened. She frowned and pressed the *repeat* key to hear the message again. Then for a third time — and a fourth.

Slowly, she set the phone aside and lay back in her chair, staring at the ceiling. Becky needed her. Should she go? What was left here, to stay for? The play was over, the supermarket could manage fine without her — a simple message would handle that.

But, if she went, was she running away? She who prided herself on never running away from anything? To stay true to herself, she should stay and fight her corner — yet how do you fight a ghost? Least of all, when it wasn't the ghost who was at fault, but the people who were left behind.

You can't help people who don't want help.

Kathy had faced down every problem in her life — but never one which hurt her half as badly as this one.

She hated dithering. Leave, or stay? Accept, or refuse? She placed her glass with a click on the table, picking up the phone. *Contacts.* She scrolled rapidly down to Becky's number, and pressed the dialling key.

Away up north, another mobile phone began to ring.

9

Becky sat in May sunshine on the fence at the bus stop, enjoying the warmth on her face — a face now deeply tanned. In her jeans and almost-best T-shirt, her hair spilling over her shoulders and with the wind blowing through it, she looked like a gypsy at home in the scene. About a mile away, the first grey stone houses of the village showed amid green hedgerows. Behind her, the blue hills of the Dales rose to a sparkling sky of clouds and sunshine.

She screened her eyes, peering down the dusty road, then pushed herself onto her feet to wait, hands on hips. An indicator flashed, and the Blackburn bus drew up, in a smell of hot oil and rubber tyres. The door swished open, to show Kathy waiting at the steps leading down to the door.

'I'll take your travel bag,' Becky said, reaching up.

The two women embraced, as the bus pulled away.

'Look at you!' said Kathy. 'You're straight out of a holiday poster.'

Becky noted that her friend's normally

lively face was shadowed. 'A good trip up?' she asked.

'I can't believe how many buses I've been on,' said Kathy. 'Or how many times I've had to ask directions. This place wasn't easy to find.'

Becky smiled. 'Wrong transport mode. If you'd come by narrowboat, there was only one long canal between us. Now we've only half a mile to go, down the towpath here.'

Kathy paused, looking over the fields to the hills beyond.

'Wow!' she said. 'What are these?'

'The Yorkshire Dales. We've been here so long, I scarcely see them now. Unless I take a trip away from them . . . when I feel there's a hole in the scenery, until they're back in place and I'm home.'

'No need to ask if you like it here.'

'I love it — the place and the people.'

'You're like a new woman.' Kathy's eyes turned shrewd. 'Sometimes that means a new man?'

Becky shrugged defensively.

'Who is he?' Kathy asked. 'Where is he? More important, when do I get to meet him?'

Becky coloured. 'He might drop in tonight — he's working in Skipton.'

'Doing what?'

'Repairing narrowboats. You passed his

place, down at Foulridge.'

'Sounds nasty.'

'Anything but. It's a lovely little village, with a gorgeous common green.'

'Look at these ducklings.' Kathy pointed, enchanted. Four or five fluffy little brown birds scampered easily over lily leaves at the edge of the canal.

'You see all sorts of birds here,' said Becky. 'We've even a resident heron, who pretends he's a sparrow when we're putting out food.'

'No wonder you like it here. Is that your boat?'

'That's us. And that threadbare old scarecrow draped over a chair on the roof and reading a book is Noel. Your Ancient Mariner.'

'Has he been . . . ?'

'He's a tower of strength, a pillar holding up the sky. From the day we set off, he's quietly come to life again, and been the substitute dad I always knew — for myself and Jon.'

'Where is Jon?'

'Up in the village, playing football.'

'No bullying?'

'Not him. He's the star of the school team.'

'So your lives have been transformed — and it's not just this new job in the village school?'

'Absolutely. But wait till you see the school.

You'll fall in love with it, an old-fashioned schoolhouse, with everything but a handbell to bring in its pupils, and real blackboards and chalk inside. It's like working in a museum — until you find out that the kids are razor sharp. They're getting the same education they would at a posh private school. It's something out of a Thomas Armstrong book, the life's work of a quirky old guy who is in his late seventies, and a head teacher who has dedicated herself to perfection.'

'Stop terrifying me.'

'You'll love Pop, he's a gem. But you won't see Liza for a bit, until she's recovered from her surgery.'

'Until then, we'll be bossed around by you?'

'Exactly. A benevolent despot — or I would be, if I could only get a couple of hours more sleep at night. You have no idea of the paperwork for this inspection — bureaucracy gone mad!'

'Can I help?'

'No. Liza and I have it under control. She dictates from her hospital bed, and I rush back to fill in the next few forms, before I forget. Henrietta is giving you a room in her house — rent free.'

'That's good.'

Kathy's head was down. She had slowed almost to a standstill.

Becky took her arm gently. 'What's up, Kathy?'

The dark head came up, the brown eyes full of misery.

'You're so happy,' Kathy whispered. 'And I'm glad.'

'You don't look it. What's wrong?'

'Everything.'

Becky waited. 'I could use a list,' she prompted gently. 'Then I can worry with you. What's happened?'

The brown eyes filled. 'Oh, Becky,' she said brokenly. 'I've made such a hash of everything, and it's too late to go back and put it right. My life is a total, utter mess. I don't know where else to turn — so I've turned to you . . . '

★ ★ ★

Becky walked along the hospital corridor, stifling a yawn. The relentless pressure of teaching, preparing, and working long past midnight on paperwork for the inspection, was beginning to tell. But they were almost home now, on the self assessment marathon. She paused outside the door of the side ward, for which Henrietta had insisted on paying,

214

gathering her energies.

The nurse looked up from tidying the bed, and saw the armful of papers. 'It's flowers or grapes you're supposed to be bringing,' she scolded. 'Not more work for her to do.'

'She's doing the work,' argued Liza. 'I'm only lying here, and making suggestions. Where are yesterday's forms, Becky? I'll run through these, before we start on parent involvement.'

Becky sidled towards the nurse, as Liza began to read. 'How is she, really?' she asked quietly.

'I can hear,' said Liza. 'She's perfectly well, thank you. I like what you've done here, Becky — just a change of wording, but it makes it sound more positive.'

'She's fine,' the nurse finally managed to reply. 'But not as fit and well as she would like to think she is. And I wish she'd stop behaving like a schoolmistress, and realize that she's only a patient, needing rest.'

'Stuff and nonsense!' came from the bed.

The nurse rolled her eyes. 'God help her staff!' she said. 'I'm off.'

The ward door closed.

'She means well,' said Liza. 'But she's such a fusspot.'

'She's also, for the moment, your boss . . . '

'In her dreams!' snapped Liza. 'Did you

215

print out the parent forms for the last inspection from my computer?'

'Yes. I was so tired, I almost forgot your password. Then it came back — *MaisieD.*' Becky glanced at Liza, who looked drained and low. On instinct, she asked: 'Just who is or was MaisieD?'

Liza smiled, leaning back on her pillows. 'A beloved old spinster aunt we all adored. When our mums died, she took over as their substitute and watched over us. If we got into trouble, she was fighting like a sister, at our sides. She lived until she was ninety-four, and held our family together. There are times when I miss her still.' She glanced up. 'That Mike of yours — he seems a nice lad?'

Becky blinked. 'He is. I am very fond of him.'

'And?'

Becky coloured. 'With one failed marriage behind me — even if it started with the best of intentions — I'm not rushing into anything. I couldn't go through all that heartbreak again — nor would I want to bring more misery on Jon. Now, what about these forms?'

Liza ignored her. 'That old aunt of mine,' she smiled. 'She was always warning me not to do what she'd done — telling me I should let my heart rule my head when it mattered, not the other way round. She said I was so busy looking out for bowler hats in the crowd, that I was letting all the bonnets go past. It wasn't true, of course. I simply never met a man who swept me off my feet. But maybe her advice has some value — about listening to your heart, as well as your head?'

She picked up the forms, skimming through the content. 'We can use most of this. Just freshen up the words a little, as you've been doing . . . these three sections we must update, because we've changed how we bring parents into project-work design . . . '

The visiting hour sped past; while Liza dictated, Becky scribbled and came up with counter suggestions. When the bell sounded to mark the ending of the visiting hour, Becky sat back and wriggled cramped fingers.

'That's only the final summary forms to complete,' Liza said wearily. 'I want to use your words and thinking as much as possible there, to give a totally fresh feel to the submission. I couldn't have done this without you, Becky. Pop is excellent, but has his limitations.'

'And we couldn't have done it without you. Pop's been guiding the teaching side, helping Kathy to take your class. That's left me free, to work on this. So it's been a real team effort.'

'How is Kathy coping?'

'Brilliantly. She's taken to multi-group teaching like a duck to water.'

'Excellent.' Liza hesitated. 'Well, thanks for coming. It's nice to see a face I know — Henrietta means well, but the privacy of a side ward is balanced by lying here for hours on my own, staring at the four walls.'

'A couple of days, and you'll be home.' Becky suspected that Liza would have been home already, if there had been anyone to look after her.

'I'm looking forward to that — now, don't miss your bus.'

'No, Miss.'

'Stop — what do you call teasing nowadays? — winding me up.'

'Yes, Miss.'

'Stop it! And, Becky . . .' The older woman coloured again. 'I just want you to know . . . I feel privileged. Privileged to have been working with my successor. You were born to do this job. With me to coach you, Henrietta's school will pass into safe hands, when I retire. Which is a huge weight off my mind.'

Becky stared at her, unable to reply.

'Thank you,' she said finally. 'And Liza, get well again — for all of us.'

★ ★ ★

The wind rattled the letter box outside the flat. David juggled the car keys in his hand, waiting while Sally struggled into her coat. There was a frown of irritation on his normally patient face, so symptomatic of recent weeks that it made Sally clumsier still.

At last the coat was on. Uncomfortable across her shoulders, but she'd wriggled long enough. She hastily buttoned it up. 'Ready, Daddy,' she said.

She had to say it twice, before it registered. 'Oh, right,' he said. 'Let's go.'

Sally stuck her hands deep into her pockets and tried discreetly to pull the coat into a more comfortable fit. It didn't work. She stopped, frowning, in the open doorway and looking at the crumpled piece of paper in her hand.

'Oh, do hurry!' snapped David. 'We're late.'

Sally barely heard him: she was reading Kathy's note.

She looked up, holding it out dumbly to her father.

'What is it?' he asked. Then his eyes picked up the writing: *Sally — I told you that you would be our star. At least I got that bit right. Kathy.*

His car keys dropped to the floor.

'Where did you find this?' he asked hoarsely.

'In my pocket. She must have slipped it

there, when she disappeared after the performance. And wasn't back home, when we went round to see her.'

David stared at the note, smoothing its crushed edges.

'You love her, don't you?' Sally asked.

He looked up, then what he was going to say to fudge the situation died on his tongue. He nodded silently.

'Is that why you have been so crabby, these last two weeks?'

'Have I?' David picked up his keys. 'Sorry, Sal,' he said. 'Yes, I love her — I've been miserable since we had the row.'

'Over me?'

David shrugged. 'Over both of us. We made things impossible for her — it's been so difficult, adjusting to living after your mum died.'

She came over to take his hand, in an instinctive role reversal.

'Mum's dead,' she said. 'We can't change that. I've tried.'

'Me too. Hundreds of times. Wakening up, dreaming it was a mistake . . . that there was a simple explanation of why she'd simply dropped out of our lives.'

'Then you waken, and it feels so bad. Like she has just died again.'

David nodded numbly. 'You too?' he asked.

'All the time.'

A silence grew, lengthened.

'So, what are we going to do about it?' he finally asked.

Tears rolled down Sally's cheeks. 'Accept that Mum's dead,' she said.

'And then?'

'I don't know. Only that we can't bring her back. And that what Kathy shouted, that time, was true. Mum wouldn't have wanted us to bury ourselves beside her, stop living. So we have to start again, and learn to live without her. And maybe that means letting other people into where she once was, in our hearts.'

David looked quizzically at his daughter. 'Deep thoughts for a 10-year-old,' he said quietly.

'Not mine, from Mum's favourite symphony,' she replied. 'Mahler's *Symphony Number 2* — 'Death, and Resurrection' — where the melody comes out from the darkness, and steps into sunshine again. Mum was always playing that to me.'

He found himself smiling. 'How do you remember all this?'

'Because what she taught is all I have left of her.'

David wrapped his arms tightly around his daughter. They hugged in gentle silence, until she pushed herself away.

'Kathy was right about me,' she said. 'I loved every minute of being up there, on stage, and singing. Maybe she's right about you too. Maybe Mum sent her here, to look after both of us, because she couldn't bear to watch us struggling on our own.'

He tried to gather her back into his arms again, unable to speak.

She pushed herself away. 'Well?' she demanded. 'What are you going to do about it?'

'Perhaps it's too late,' said David. 'The damage done.'

'Think Mahler,' she told him. 'Life always triumphs over death. Love never dies. Have you Kathy's phone number?'

David grimaced. 'We always started arguing, before we got that far.'

She pushed him through the door. 'Come on,' she said. 'Let's drive over to her supermarket. We can ask them if they have her contact number. Refuse to leave, until they tell us. She won't just have run away.'

David spun her round. 'Sally,' he said, 'Kathy was right about you. You *are* a star — and not just on stage.'

★   ★   ★

After school, Becky found Kathy leaning on the bridge across the canal and staring up at the hills. 'Haven't you got used to them yet?' she teased.

Kathy jumped. 'Sorry, what did you say?'

Becky leaned on the low stone bridge beside her. 'Why don't you phone him?' she asked quietly. 'He must be wondering where you are.'

'We never got round to swapping phone numbers,' Kathy said.

'I can't believe that!'

'It's true. We were either running, or visiting . . . or having a row.'

'So how does he get in touch? Or how do you get in touch with him?'

Kathy shrugged. 'I'm not really ready for that yet,' she mumbled.

'One day, one of you is going to have to make the effort.'

Kathy turned away. 'I'm going for a run,' she said. 'To clear my head of chalk dust and fretting about the inspection.'

Becky sighed. When you're happy and have found someone who fills your mind and heart, you want the whole world to be happy too. Especially your best friend. 'The Pennine Way goes through the village,' she said. 'I don't know how rough the track is, but people cycle it. And it would take you up into the hills.'

'Fine,' said Kathy. 'More form-filling tonight?'

'No — thank goodness. I'll drop in and check Liza doesn't need anything, then get home and start cooking our supper. It's Noel's night off. He and Henrietta are away to listen to a choir in Skipton tonight.'

'In her coal lorry?' A brave but hollow echo of Kathy's normal quick humour.

'I'd love to see them turning up in that! No, she has the use of a friend's ancient car as well. Mike's dropping in, for supper — like to join us?'

'Three's company — four's a crowd.'

'Don't be daft — come along. You can prepare for tomorrow's classes later — that's what I'll be doing.'

'Maybe.' Kathy turned from the bridge. 'I'm off to climb into my running gear.' She hesitated. 'Becky — Mike is just about perfect for you. Make sure you get and keep his phone number . . . '

'I already have,' said Becky. 'It's in my phone, it's written down — and it's memorized. A real belt-and-braces job!'

* * *

'What's Mike carrying?' Jonathon asked, crossing the cabin and peering eagerly through the towpath windows. 'It's a bike!'

He had exploded up the cabin steps and was out before Becky turned. She dried her hands, leaned forward to look through the windows, sighed, and went up to meet Mike. A well-used boy's bike was draped over the broad shoulders, the frame and wheel rims cleaned until the sunlight glinted off them.

'What have you done now?' she asked resignedly.

'It was going to waste,' Mike said. 'Her kid had grown out of it, and it was rusting in her garden. She was glad to sell it to me. It only cost a few pounds,' he added. 'My pleasure.'

Jonathon was jumping all over him, like an eager spaniel. 'It's perfect!' he shouted. 'And it has real gears.'

'It's a Ridgeback MX20, twist-handle *Derailluer*,' Mike told him. 'A really good make,' he added to Becky. 'Years of solid use and wear in it. I'll get some cycle paint and we can touch up the chips on the frame. But it's all checked over and greased, with new brake blocks fitted.'

Becky shook her head. 'You're spoiling him,' she said. 'You, and Noel.'

Mike grinned. 'You asked me to help him fit in at school. All boys have bikes — they'll be living on them over the summer holidays. So it's part of the treatment . . . ' He was watching Jonathon swoop along the path, turn and head back, skidding to a halt on the clay of the path. 'That saddle needs raising.'

'No. It's fine,' protested Jonathon.

'It's not a BMX for trick work, it's a proper cycle. You need to be able to straighten your legs as you pedal, or you'll cramp. Bring it over . . . watch, this is how you release the saddle . . . that lever, open it, like this. Takes off the clamp pressure, and lets you ease the shank out. See?'

The two heads were close together, absorbed in the work. Boys' toys. In her mind, Becky put in the apostrophe for plural.

Then Jonathon was off in a shower of grit.

'What am I going to do with you, Mike?' she demanded.

'Marry me.'

Becky's heart stopped. 'Is that a proposal?'

'No, you're not ready yet. Take it as a final warning. When the real proposal comes, I want candlelight and gypsy violinists, while I go down on one knee — that had better be my good one — and ask you over our shared bag of fish and chips.'

'With salt and vinegar? No expense spared?'

'You can even have pickled onion,' he offered.

'No onion,' she said firmly. 'You're not buying my favours that way.'

The laughing grey eyes became serious. 'That wasn't what the bike was about,' he said firmly. 'That was between Jon and me.'

'I know.'

She threw her arms round him, felt a hug which drove the breath from her body, then a gentle pat on the back.

'What's for dinner?' he asked.

'A surprise,' she said. 'As Noel will be surprised, when he comes home. I've been checking out where the fairies are leaving his booze and, do you know, there was a bottle of Shiraz waiting for us there.'

'Fairies think of everything,' Mike said solemnly.

★ ★ ★

Kathy had run until she was ready to drop, along the narrow country lane leading onto the broad track which was the Pennine Way, up through fields and moorland, until she was high in the hills she had seen from Longbank. She stopped, set her hands on her knees and gasped for air. At the best of times, this would have taxed her severely, because she was more used to running on the flat, where speed and not strength was the essence. However, this was not the best of times and she had pushed herself mercilessly, trying to exorcize her demons.

She felt the buzzer of her mobile phone tickle through her tracksuit pocket, then came the ringtone, rising in volume. Becky?

Kathy fumbled out the phone, glanced at the number. Unknown.

'Hello? Kathy?'

It was a young girl's voice. She recognized it instantly.

'Sally?'

'Yes — it's me.'

'Is something wrong?' Kathy couldn't believe the sense of panic she was feeling. 'Has something happened to your dad?'

'He's fine. He's here. He wants to talk to you . . . I found your note. Oh, Kathy, you were right about so many things. Why did you go away and leave us?'

Tears streamed down Kathy's face. She fought for words, found silence.

'Daddy wants to speak to you. Come back, please.'

It was just as well the mobile phone was made of rugged materials, or it would have snapped in Kathy's hand. A new voice came . . .

'Kathy? Where are you? Are you all right?'

'I'm up on the Pennine Way,' she told him. 'Sweating out my troubles.'

'You've been pushing hard. I can hear your breathing.'

'Thin, clear air — and you should have seen the climb.'

'I can imagine. But where are you?'

'The back of beyond. A tiny place called Longbank, in North Yorks.'

'What are you doing up there? Why did you leave? We had a heck of a job, getting the supermarket to release your mobile number. The manager wouldn't give it; we only got it because one of the supervisors took a chance.'

'Jean?'

'I don't know her name, but she'd seen us collecting you before.'

A silence. High up over Kathy's head a buzzard wheeled round and round, in a thermal. Her mind felt as if it was going round in circles too.

'I got a phone call from a friend,' she finally said. 'They needed a teacher in the village school. There's inspectors coming, and the head teacher was taken into hospital. They were in a mess and I came here to help her out.'

Another silence. 'How long will you be away, then?'

'I don't know.'

The buzzard, now a tiny dot in the sky, glided away from its thermal towards the far end of the valley. Putting more distance between itself, and her. Was there a message for her in this?

'Are you still there, Kathy?' he asked.

'Yes.'

'Sally's right. We need you here. It's going to take the three of us, to sort out where we go from here. Try to find our way from the darkness and back to the sunshine again. Please come home and let's talk it through.'

Kathy searched for her buzzard. It was gone. Like her tongue.

'Kathy — I love you, dearly. I need you here. Things will be different, so much better, now.'

She should have leapt into the air with joy. Instead, that now-familiar leaden feeling settled over her, despair where there should have been delight, doubt and depression where there should have been joy.

'I can't,' she finally whispered. 'I'm too messed up. I need time and space, to sort myself out. To think through where I am, and what I want to do with my life. I've never felt so confused and lost. Anyway, I can't come now — can't leave the others when they're depending on me. Not with the inspectors due within the week. I'm sorry, David. I can't come back — even if there weren't any inspectors due, I still wouldn't know what to say, how to handle us. Let me sort myself out . . . '

Eyes blurring, she closed her mobile phone

and switched it off.

No buzzard, anywhere. Right now, it felt as if it had taken away all hope with it. Why did she feel this way? Why cut him off, when he was saying the very words she ached to hear? Didn't she want to go back and help David and Sally to build a new life?

A life that included her?

Kathy thrust the phone into her tracksuit pocket, and zipped it up. She looked at the track ahead, a rough mix of gravel and dried-out mud, weaving in and out of the rocks and boulders. Climbing ever higher, towards the blue sky. Once, she would have been unable to resist the challenge. But that day was over — and a new day had not yet begun.

Kathy turned wearily away and began to run downhill, stumbling, because her eyes were looking but not seeing where she was going.

★   ★   ★

'What are you doing here, Noel?' Becky demanded.

The tall frame ambled alongside her and leaned against the wall of the schoolhouse. 'Solidarity,' Noel said. 'And there might be a scoop in it for me.'

' 'School inspectors arrest temporary staff'?'

'I was thinking more along the lines of

'Coal merchant bags Ofsted inspectors.''

'Don't,' said Henrietta. 'I'm struggling to keep my breakfast down.'

'Relax,' said Pop. 'The school hasn't changed, and until now we've always won top grades. So let's simply go in there and teach. Right, Kathy?'

Henrietta craned her neck. 'That's not them, surely,' she said. 'It's the village taxi. Who . . . ?'

The taxi drew up at the school gates, and kids crowded round the school railings to watch. The driver came out, and helped an ashen-faced Liza Forbes through its doors.

'Oh, Lord,' groaned Henrietta. 'Wait here. I'll send her home.'

'Fiddlesticks,' said Liza. 'I heard you, Henrietta Yates. This is my school too. Why has the bell not been sounded? Why are the children not in line?'

'Oops!' said Pop. He disappeared, and the school bell rang.

'Stop fussing, Henrietta. I'm perfectly fine,' snapped Liza.

She reached the steps as the children lined up meekly in front of her. Liza surveyed them, as Wellington once must have studied his troops, then her back straightened, and she became every inch a head teacher.

'We have inspectors coming today, children.'

Her calm voice carried over every inch of the schoolyard. 'We are going to show them that this is a very special school. For you, as for your parents and grandparents. You are carrying a brave torch for tradition, and you will not let us down. You will behave quite normally, answering any questions you are asked promptly, telling the inspectors calmly and clearly what you know — which means no sudden flights of fancy, Deborah Fotheringham . . . '

This brought a snicker of laughter from the kids, and Deborah beamed.

'Now, quietly into your classrooms. Lessons start in two minutes' time.'

Liza turned to Kathy and Pop. 'Take the two classes, please. Becky and myself will handle the Chief Inspector. Henrietta, stop fidgeting.'

'I'm nervous,' Henrietta said.

'Nonsense! What is there to be nervous about? Here they come.'

A line of three private cars turned slowly into the village street and drove towards the school. Liza waited on the steps, her head spinning behind her stoic and determined stance. Two men and a woman got out, and walked through the schoolyard to meet them.

'I'm Miss Forbes,' she said. 'Head teacher of this school. Please follow me to my study, where you can tell us how you would like to run this inspection. Henrietta, could you organize us some tea, please?'

The coal merchant stopped in her tracks, then a wry smile came onto her taut face. 'Yes, Miss,' she said — and ignored the scathing look this drew from Liza. Worth it, she thought gleefully. Feeling pretty much the urchin-in-trouble that she'd always been, when she was being taught here as a child.

About half an hour later, the Ofsted Chief Inspector spread out the detailed paperwork underpinning the visit, the forms Liza and Becky had slaved over for weeks.

'Everything that we need is here,' he said quietly. 'But, before we start, I feel bound to give you some advice. With your two core staff incapacitated on grounds of ill health, and the current teaching programme in the hands of young temporary teachers, you are entitled to ask for a postponement of the inspection. You appear to have coped admirably, and the children's education has not suffered. But this formal inspection, once launched, must be carried out in a thorough and objective manner, no allowance made. I can easily refer back, and ask Ofsted to set a new date — probably in the autumn term. By then, you will have reorganized yourselves, and Miss Forbes will be fully fit and in post.'

Henrietta looked at Liza Forbes. Who didn't bat an eye.

'I have every confidence in my school,' she said calmly. 'I have total trust in the quality and diligence of the staff who have been preparing the children for this inspection. I see no reason whatsoever, why the inspection should be postponed.'

'Miss Yates, as Chairperson of the Trust?'

Henrietta swallowed. 'I agree with Miss Forbes. We are ready to be inspected, and look forward with confidence to the grade you will give us.'

The Chief Inspector nodded. 'Very well,' he said quietly. 'My colleagues will enter both your classrooms, while I shall start to take you rigorously through the Self Evaluation case that you have submitted to Ofsted. Can we begin, please?'

10

Liza Forbes was struggling: the waves of dizziness were getting stronger, more frequent. Please not now, she pleaded silently . . . not here.

'Liza! Are you all right?' Henrietta's voice cut across the Chief Inspector's last question, just as Liza's head dropped forward. Becky caught her, when she slumped sideways in her chair.

The Chief Inspector glanced over his glasses, and promptly swept their joint paperwork to the side, clearing the tabletop. 'Lift her onto the table,' he said, his voice calm and authoritative. 'Get her head at the same level as her body — she's fainted. Here . . . let me.'

He took Liza's body from Becky, lifting and laying her down onto the table top. Taking one of her hands, he gently patted her face. 'Miss Forbes? Miss Forbes?'

'I'll get cold water,' Henrietta said, flying from the room.

'She'll be fine — she's coming round.'

Liza's eyelids fluttered, then opened to stare dazedly at the ceiling, and the faces looking down on her. Weakly, she tried to roll over and rise but was gently pushed back by the Chief Inspector.

'Stay there,' he told her. 'Let the blood flow back into your brain.'

Henrietta erupted into the room, with a glass of fresh water and a towel which left a trail of drips on the floor. 'Is she . . . ?'

'She's fine,' said Becky, holding one of Liza's hands.

'She shouldn't have come here,' Henrietta scolded. 'She wasn't fit.'

Liza didn't have the strength to answer back; nevertheless colour was returning to her face. She tried again to rise, and was held down gently for a second time by the Chief Inspector.

'Let the blood circulate yet,' he said. 'Don't rush.'

'I'm perfectly fine,' Liza protested weakly.

'You're anything but . . . ' Henrietta snapped. 'I'm taking you home, whether you like it or not . . . '

'But the inspection . . . '

Becky squeezed Liza's hand. 'You've drilled me through every sentence of our submission; and what I can't answer, Henrietta or Pop will know. We'll manage. Let Henrietta take you home — you're in no fit state to answer questions.'

'I'll phone for a taxi,' Henrietta said.

'Here, take my car.' The Chief Inspector produced a well-worn set of keys. 'It's all right,' he smiled. 'It's an old Volvo — built like a tank and indestructible.'

He eased Liza semi-upright and she struggled to sit up. 'Easy, easy,' he chided. 'Give yourself time — or you'll just flake out again.'

He helped Liza down onto her feet. She swayed, but Henrietta's sturdy frame propped her up.

'Leave me alone, Henrietta,' she said. 'Stop fussing.'

'Do what you're told, for once . . . ' But Henrietta was gentleness itself, as she half-steered, half-carried Liza from the room.

The door closed behind them.

'A well-matched team,' the Chief Inspector smiled.

'They are. There's no better head teacher in the land for a school like this, than Miss Forbes. And nobody will fight harder for the school, its pupils and its staff, than Henr — Miss Yates.'

Gathering his forms, the Chief Inspector arranged them carefully across the table. 'I'm an ex-soldier,' he said quietly. 'I respect courage, wherever I find it, and in whatever form it takes. These two ladies of yours have a wonderful reputation that has reached even Ofsted. They are the heart and soul of this small school. Long may that continue.'

He glanced up, apologetically. 'However, now that we've started the inspection process, I have no other option but to complete it — but not until the Chairperson of the Trust has returned. So we have a choice . . . ' The frosty blue eyes twinkled. 'We can sit in silence for the next twenty minutes, or go off the record, be human, and have a chat. I vote for chatting. Tell me, how did you find adjusting to multiple-group teaching, after all your training and experience of much larger classes?'

Becky hesitated: there is no such thing as a free dinner, and perhaps off-the-record chats fell into the same category.

'Hey,' the Chief Inspector smiled. 'There's no Dictaphone running, no hidden cameras, no newspaper stings. I asked, because when I started teaching myself, it was in Northumbria. My first class had six pupils in it — each at a different stage. It was like preparing for six classes, every day, until I found a way to pick a topic that I could teach at six different levels. I was there for eight years, and they were the happiest years of my life. My wife keeps telling me to go back and pick up a stick of chalk again . . . '

Becky laughed. 'We've plenty of chalk, feel free.'

She found herself talking, liking the man. They chatted through the teaching issues of how best to merge curricula. She found herself telling him how Pop and Liza had dropped in, the first few days — not so much to check on what she was doing, as to make sure that she was coping and not needing help. 'It was like having two guardian angels, watching over you,' she finished.

'How did you handle all the quasi-religious stuff that Cluny the founder brought with him into the school?' he asked thoughtfully.

'Pop — Mr Bailey — took that at first. Then I got interested, sat in on the discussions, and we've taken joint seminars from that point on. It's the most interesting material I've ever taught. And these children are young enough to be completely open-minded. For generations, this school has turned out pupils who understand and accept sociocultural material from all around the world — leaving them able to see exactly where other nations are coming from, so that they can mix and work with people from other cultures. That can only be good.'

The Chief Inspector nodded. 'As a soldier, I served throughout the world and our narrow-minded attitude often appalled me.

We have no monopoly of truth — or the right to rule others . . . '

'Who hasn't?' Henrietta pushed through the doors, handing over the car keys. 'No fresh dents that I'm aware of,' she said. 'Thanks.'

'Is Liza . . . ?' Becky asked.

'Tucked up in bed, protesting. A hot-water bottle beside her and a cup of tea and some biscuits within reach.' Henrietta slipped back into her seat at the table. 'Liza Forbes has willingly given her life to this school. It's my responsibility, as Chairperson, to make sure she doesn't do that too literally. Where are we?'

The Chief Inspector smiled. 'Waiting for you, ma'am,' he said.

'Right,' said Henrietta. 'I'm here. Fire away!'

* * *

'Oh, for Heaven's sake,' snapped Liza. 'Stop fussing, I'm *not* an invalid.' She flapped a hand at Henrietta, who was tucking a travelling rug around her in the chair. Henrietta ignored her completely, and carried on.

'How did the inspection go?' Liza asked, over her head.

'No howlers, I think,' said Becky. 'They did the general inspection this morning, while the Chief Inspector went through our submission with Henrietta and myself. Then he picked

241

about twenty issues, where his team could check the accuracy of our claims during the afternoon. And while the other two were ticking off these points with Pop's and Kathy's classes, we held our meeting with the parents from our PTA and he systematically took them through how we had developed their greater level of involvement in school policy. They did us proud.'

'And?' Liza frowned, furious with herself for failing to last the course.

'Then they packed away their pens and papers, shook our hands, smiled nicely, and drove off. Job done.'

'No hints of their decision?'

'Is there ever?' Henrietta grumbled. 'They leave you to chew your nails, and wait. It will be weeks, before we know.'

'If there was anything doubtful, the Chief Inspector would have surely probed it further,' Liza murmured. 'No follow-up questions? He didn't come back to check anything, did he?'

Becky shook her head. 'Just to thank us for looking after them.'

Liza turned to Kathy: 'How did things go at classroom level?' she asked.

'Easier than I expected,' Kathy said. 'The woman inspector was really nice — she sat in on my classes all morning. She and the second inspector went through the project work with me over lunchtime, and he came in to question the children about that in the afternoon. Both of them knew their teaching — they stayed quiet, and any questions they asked helped the lesson to move along. The kids were great — even Deborah. My heart was in my mouth every time they picked on her. But she was a real trouper today, never put a foot wrong.'

'Stop worrying, Liza,' Henrietta scolded.

'I'm *not* worrying. I'm simply trying to get a feel of how things went.'

The doorbell rang. 'I'll get it,' Becky said. She walked through Liza's neat hallway, and opened the door. Pop stood there, round and benign, carrying a huge box of chocolates.

'How's Liza?' he asked.

'Not well enough to eat all these.'

'Then we'll maybe have to help her.'

'Who is it?' Liza's voice came through.

'Me,' said Pop. 'I came to check that they were looking after you, and to tell you that we owe a huge debt to these two young substitutes who came on off the bench and scored for us. Here's a box of chocolates, to help you celebrate.'

'Teacher's pet,' scoffed Henrietta. 'What kind of chocolates?'

'*Her* kind of chocolates,' Pop smiled. 'Posh Belgian.'

'Drat,' said Henrietta. 'I like the ones from York.'

★   ★   ★

Kathy came running lightly down the lane, enjoying the fresh breeze and the last of the afternoon sunshine. The stress of the inspection was behind her and its tension sweated out by the run. For the first time in weeks, she felt almost at peace with herself. As if, somewhere deep in her mind, she had worked out where she stood and what she wanted from life.

A strange feeling: a decision made, without her aware of any details.

Her feet skipped lightly over the loose stones, and she felt she could run like this forever. Out of nowhere, she found herself wondering if she should try to phone David when she got home. She would have his number on her Received Calls log. She could simply scroll to that and ring, that should do it.

Or would it? Was she ready to go back to Southport and try again, knowing that the pattern might still be two steps forward, and one back — could she take that, with all its bruised feelings of anger, and frustration?

Surely, it was worth one last attempt. After all, she was fighting for her future. Her stride lengthened, bringing the village into sight. As she approached the canal, she saw a familiar car parked in the broad space between the pub and the bridge. She faltered, and came to a halt, as the car doors opened.

'What are you doing here?' she asked, her heart in her mouth.

'Waiting for you,' David said. 'We went to your school, and one of the locals said he'd seen you go off running. You're looking good.'

'I'm a mess,' said Kathy.

'Have you been up into the Dales?'

'Too easy. I've been running up the Pennine Way, among the tops.'

'Bet I would have beaten you,' he said.

'In your dreams!'

They shared their first real smile in weeks.

David came over and took her hands. 'We couldn't wait any longer. It was Sally who said that we should climb into the car and keep driving until we found you and brought you home.'

Sally had been standing behind her father. Now, she hesitated, then came slowly forward. As if she was making a huge and conscious effort to close the gap between them — a gap far wider in its emotional implications than in distance.

Instinctively, Kathy freed a hand, and held it out. The gesture seemed to take away any final barrier: Sally slipped inside and Kathy's arm went naturally around her shoulders. She squeezed gently and felt answering pressure from Sally's arms round her waist.

'Please come home,' said Sally. 'I'm sorry I was so naughty, before.'

'That goes for both of us,' smiled David.

'Me too,' said Kathy. 'I have my Irish grandmother's temper.'

They walked slowly towards the car, arms round each other.

'Will you come back, then?' asked Sally. 'I just want him happy. He's been miserable without you. Mum wouldn't have wanted that.'

Now that the decision point had come, the last shreds of doubt disappeared from Kathy's mind. This was the man she wanted to share her life with. This was the family she would be part of . . . no longer on the outside, looking in.

She tightened her arm round Sally's shoulders. 'I'll come back, if you want me as well. Not just for your dad's sake — this must be a three-way deal, covering all of us. And I want only to stand *beside* your mum — never, not ever, in front of her. She owns the first part of your life; all I ask is that you let me share the rest of it with her.'

'That makes it a four-way deal,' smiled Sally. 'So be it. Deal?'

'Deal.' Sally's arm tightened.

Kathy turned to David. 'What about you?'

David turned her gently into his arms and kissed her. 'No more stepping away and hiding, ever,' he said quietly. 'I promise. I love you and want you into every corner of my life. I'm happy to wait until you can leave your job here. So long as we know that everything's OK, and you'll come back.'

'Of course I will,' said Kathy. 'We'll make a new start, then — all four of us — and take it from there.'

'Agreed.'

Kathy wriggled free. 'But first,' she said, 'just follow me.'

She set off like the wind, sprinting over the ancient bridge across the canal and heading into the village proper.

'Where to?' he called.

She stopped, the evening sunshine like a halo round her happy face.

'To my friends,' she said. 'The best friends in the world. I want to show you off to them — let Becky see what all the fuss was about.'

Then she was gone. David sighed, stepped into the car, did a quick three-point turn, and set off in pursuit of her flying figure.

'She's like trying to hold quicksilver in your hand,' he complained.

Sally watched her father smile, felt her own heart lighten.

'Let's get there first!' she said.

★ ★ ★

'Why is Mike standing on the bank and staring at our bows?' Noel asked.

'What bows?' Becky emerged from her schoolbooks.

'The pointy end of the *Ella Mae*,' Noel explained patiently.

'I know they're the pointy end,' she said irritably.

'Well, he's staring at them.'

'Why?'

'Good,' said Noel. 'Now that you've caught up with the rest of the world, that's exactly what I was asking.'

Becky gathered up her schoolwork. 'I'll do these later.'

Noel's eyes twinkled. 'Good again,' he said.

'And now I'll go out and ask him what he's doing, staring at our boat like that.'

'Even better thinking.'

Becky climbed the steps through the open cabin door. The air was full of soaring bird-song, and she savoured the scent of wild flowers from the meadow alongside the towpath. She loved this canal-family life, had barely

248

given a thought to her flat which was rented out in Southport. One day soon, she must tell her agents to sell it — giving her the funds to buy a house in Longbank for the winter.

But not right now. The present was too precious.

'What are you looking at?' She went to Mike and confidently threaded her arm through his.

'It's a long story,' he said.

'Then come in, and tell us in the comfort of the cabin.'

Noel emerged, carrying a couple of folding chairs. 'Let's sit outside,' he said. 'It's a lovely evening, despite the midges. Too good to stay indoors.'

'Where's Jon?' Mike asked.

'Somewhere,' Becky said vaguely. 'Off on his bike, with the lads — they could be playing football, or cricket, or just cycling like mad things up into the Dales. They have more energy than they know what to do with.'

Just as it should be, Noel thought contentedly. Jon had finally cast off his wrappings of cotton wool.

Mike came up with a third chair. 'I've filled the kettle and put it on,' he said apologetically. 'In case my throat gets dry.'

'Why?' asked Noel.

'It's a long story,' Becky repeated solemnly, and stuck out her tongue at Mike's wry grin.

'Well, it is,' sighed Mike. He took a deep breath. 'I've gone and bought a boat. And because I've got a boat, I'll have to change my whole way of life — take on someone to work for me. So that I can spend some time with my boat.'

'What sort of boat?' asked Becky.

'An old canal barge. It was rescued and rebuilt as a small houseboat by my granddad — oh, about forty years ago. Then she was rescued again by my dad, about twenty years later and rebuilt as a cruiser, just like this. Now the guy who ran her is packing up . . . and gave me first refusal on her.'

'You won't regret it,' said Noel.

'I bought first, and thought second. I've never acted like that in my life before — without a second's pause or planning. Now I have to find a way to make it work.'

'You will,' said Noel. 'I'll go down, and brew the tea.'

He went down the cabin steps and they heard mugs clinking.

'I'm so glad, Mike,' said Becky. 'Both about the boat, and you getting help — you work too hard.'

'Listen to who is talking!'

Becky smiled. 'I know,' she said. 'But you do need more time to yourself. How big is she? A forty or a sixty tonner? What's her name?'

'She's bigger than the *Ella Mae*, but less than sixty tonnes,' Mike replied. 'She was named after the man's wife, but the lady died a few years ago. Now he's no longer fit enough to go through the locks himself, so he's selling up. That sort of name is personal, belongs to a private and happy past. He's taken it off the boat — painted it out — and right now, she's nameless. So I have to come up with another name that's why I was staring at your *Ella Mae* nameplate.'

'Why? Thinking of *Ella Mae II*?' asked Noel, bringing up the mugs.

'No — I had another name in mind.'

'What?' Becky asked.

'The *Rebecca C*. But that's a bit presumptuous.'

Becky swallowed. 'Nobody calls me Rebecca,' she said. 'I hate that name.'

'Then the *Becky C*.'

'Doesn't sound right for a boat,' she protested.

'Hello there, everybody.' It was Liza Forbes, out walking a determined mile along the towpath, trying to get fit again.

'Liza! Come aboard. Would you like a cup of tea? It's just made.'

The head teacher hesitated. 'That would be lovely,' she said.

Mike helped her aboard, guiding her into a

chair. Becky hopped up and sat on the edge of the cabin roof. She looked at Mike. 'Perfect! I have just the name for you,' she said. 'The *Liza F.* We're renaming a narrowboat that Mike has just bought,' she explained.

'After me?' The head teacher's thin face coloured. 'But . . . '

'Sounds absolutely perfect,' Noel said.

Mike rubbed his face. 'That's quite uncanny,' he said quietly. 'Do you know what her original name was? Back when my granddad and my dad were working on her? Her name in these old days was the *Eliza Forbisher.*'

'Why not call her that again?' said Liza. 'It's a beautiful name.'

'And her original identity,' added Becky. 'She has come back to you, completing the circle of ownership. Why not call her exactly as your grandfather did? The *Eliza Forbisher.* I love that name.'

Noel headed down the cabin steps.

'Where are you off to?' Becky called after him.

'If we're naming a boat, it's champagne we should be using,' his voice floated up from the cabin. 'It's too much to hope that the fairies have left us one of these . . . but I think they hid a Merlot in my shirt drawer.'

'Not the usual place,' Becky said *sotto voce* to Mike.

'Indeed no,' said Noel, emerging with the bottle. 'But a bad fairy must have found my usual place. Last time I went to check, a bottle of Shiraz had disappeared.'

'Maybe they took it back again?' offered Becky.

Noel's eyes crinkled. 'If they did, they left the screw cap behind,' he said.

'You can't trust fairies, nowadays,' Mike sighed sadly.

★ ★ ★

The wind from the Ribble Estuary little more than a cooling breeze, the two of them ran companionably, shoulder to shoulder. No longer competing to see who could leave the other struggling in their dust.

'I can't believe Christine has offered me my old job back,' said Kathy.

'Why not? She knows what a brilliant teacher you are. Everybody was talking about the performance you got out of the kids in the school play.' David glanced down at Kathy's slender figure, running easily at his side. 'You're building up a biggish fan club,' he smiled.

She pulled a face at him.

'It's good to have you back,' he said quietly. 'You have no idea, the gap you left in my life when you went storming off.'

'Slinking off,' she corrected. 'With my tail between my legs — because you left an even bigger gap in mine.'

'Never again,' he said. 'Either of us. Promise me that.'

'I promise.' She eased in front of him, to let some cars pass, then dropped back alongside. 'I've been thinking. Sally's voice. That's not just a little girl's voice she has — there's real quality there. Maybe that's the form Beth's musical genes are going to take. Maybe she will turn out to be a singer. You should steer her towards taking singing lessons — unless it's still too early for her voice to have settled down. Even so, she can still benefit from some sort of training . . . you should think of getting her into a really good local choir. Let her find her feet in making music, and standing on a stage in front of people. Lay the foundations.'

Kathy glanced up. 'Look, I know I'm talking out of turn,' she apologized. 'But what do you think?'

David ran for a few moments, then smiled down.

'I think it should be as much your decision, as mine,' he said.

'What does that mean?'

He caught her arm, and stopped her. Turned her gently towards him.

'You've been back a month,' he said

quietly. 'It has been one of the happiest months of my life. It's probably too early, but I'm asking you to marry me. Then we can *both* sit down with Sally, and persuade her.'

Kathy stared up at him. 'Marry you?' she asked faintly.

'Sort of. Is that too terrible to consider?'

Kathy glanced over the fence, at the mounds and rushes of the Mere.

'Last time I was here, I was crying my eyes out,' she said.

'Does that mean yes, or no?'

'It mean yes. As in yes, please. As in yes, forever.'

Cars hooted as they stood locked together, kissing. Neither of them heard, nor saw, the smiling occupants.

Finally Kathy pushed him away, and turned to hare back into Southport.

'Rats!' he sighed. 'Here we go again . . . '

It took him almost a mile to catch up. 'What are you doing? Where are you going?' he panted.

'Back home, to tell Sally,' Kathy said.

And poured on even more speed.

★ ★ ★

'This had better be important, Liza. Oh . . . ' Henrietta stopped inside the door of Liza's

255

study, her eyes fixed on the sealed letter that was lying in front of the head teacher.

'Is it?' she asked.

Liza nodded. 'I've asked the other two to send the children out for an early playtime,' she said quietly. 'They should be here at any minute . . . Ah, the bell.'

She smiled as the children rampaged out of the old building, their clamour receding down the school corridor and fading into the distance of the playground outside. Most of Liza's life had been spent with that background noise. She wouldn't have changed a single moment of it.

'I want everybody here,' she said. 'The whole team.'

'Absolutely,' said a coal-stained Henrietta, eyes fixed on the letter.

A gentle knock on the door, then it opened. It was Pop, with Becky at his heels. Their eyes too were drawn to the letter on Liza's desk. Pop sighed, waved Becky through, then closed the door gently behind them.

For a couple of minutes, everybody stared at the letter.

'Well, you open it,' Henrietta said. 'You're head teacher.'

'You open it,' said Liza. 'You're Chair of the Trust.'

'My hands are mucky.'

Liza reached into a desk drawer and brought out a slender letter-knife. She slid its blade carefully into the top of the envelope, then firmly cut across the edge of the envelope flap. With hands that shook, she laid down the knife and reached inside to draw out two folded sheets of A4 paper.

'There's usually only one,' muttered Henrietta.

Gathering her courage, Liza eased opened the sheets. Her eyes skimmed down the first sheet, where the Ofsted letter heading was very prominent.

'Well?' asked Henrietta, in anguished tones.

Silently, Liza slid the Ofsted letter across the desk.

'Tell me,' Henrietta whispered, face white beneath the coal dust.

'*Outstanding*,' Liza said quietly. '*Outstanding*, once again. We did it!'

Henrietta sank weakly into a chair. A single tear left a white channel down her plump cheek. 'This school is blessed,' she said quietly. 'Old Cluny sits up on his cloud, working all our strings. He found us Becky, he brought us Kathy, when we needed her most. And, together, we did it somehow. The precious independence of his school is safe again — with a grade far higher than any other local school has got.'

'What's on the other sheet?' Becky asked.

'The handwritten note.'

Liza glanced down. 'It's from the Chief Inspector,' she said. 'Hoping that I'm fully fit again.' She looked up. 'How is Kathy?' she asked, thinking of the missing team member, now that the result was through.

'She's got her old job back,' said Becky. 'And she's getting married in the summer. It's all come good for her as well.'

'I'm glad,' sighed Liza.

'Me too,' said Pop. He turned to Henrietta. 'Crisis is over,' he said. 'You've found my successor in Becky. Liza's back in post. Can I retire now? Please?'

'NO!!!' Henrietta, Liza and Becky shouted, in chorus.

'Oh, all right then,' said Pop. 'I'll carry on.'

*   *   *

'Hello? Anyone in?' Becky had tracked Mike down to the one boat in the yard which had no name.

His tousled head emerged through its cabin door.

'Becky! What a nice surprise,' he said. 'Come aboard and I'll show you round. I've been working on her all afternoon — I opened the doors to air her, and finished up renewing both sets of door frames and

258

putting in new locks. While the rest of my work gathers dust, outside. Is this the shape of things to come?'

'She looks absolutely gorgeous,' said Becky.

'Wait until you see her finished,' Mike smiled.

He steadied her as she stepped aboard, and somehow they finished up in each other's arms. 'We'll have the neighbours talking,' he said indistinctly, a few moments later. 'I saw Mrs Thing's curtains twitch, over there.'

'Let them,' said Becky.

Mike held her at arm's length. 'You look great,' he said.

'That's what travelling twelve miles in a crowded bus does for you.'

'I'd have fetched you in the van, if you'd phoned.'

'Wanted to surprise you.'

'You certainly did. What's in your bags?'

'Another surprise. I'll leave them here. Where's that guided tour you promised me?'

'If you put me down, I'll make a start on it.'

'Me, put you down? You kissed me first!'

'And last . . . ' he said, a moment later.

Down in the cabin was a small world of its own. A long, wood-panelled kitchen-cum-lounge/dinette, with an iron stove. Three neat forward bedroom cabins — a main bedroom and two singles. Then open doors out onto the bows.

'The previous owner must have loved her to bits,' said Becky. 'She's immaculate. You could live and travel anywhere in her; there's more space than the *Ella Mae*. But I don't like these curtains.'

'No. I'm taking them down and lifting out the carpets. I want to re-carpet her and reupholster her throughout. She's in great nick, but a bit of maintenance work on furnishing and fittings will restore her to good-as-new. She deserves that — it's a solid old hull, and an engine which will still be running in fifty years' time.'

'So, you're pleased with her?'

'Over the moon. But I'll need your help in choosing the upholstery, then matching the carpets, curtains, wallpaper. Creating the whole ambience for living in her, from scratch. We'll search round the textile places in Bradford, once you're on your school holidays.'

'Won't you be busy then?'

'Yes, but I'm taking on an old trade friend over the summer. He can cover for me, when I want time off. Should have done it years ago.'

She slipped an arm round him. 'Hungry?' she asked.

'Not half! But there's no food in my flat. We'll have to eat at the pub.'

'That's taken care of,' she said.

'Ah — is that what's in your bags?'

'How about eating here? Having the first picnic in your own boat?'

Mike glanced around. 'She's pretty dusty,' he objected. 'And all that sawing and sanding today didn't help.'

'I can clean that up.'

'There's no water in her tanks yet,' Mike protested. 'And I haven't checked out his dishes.'

'I've brought my own. Go and get a shower. I'll set things up.'

'Let me help you.'

'Go! Now!' Becky pushed him up the cabin stairs.

'Ten minutes,' he said.

'Take thirty. I want everything ready for you coming back.'

'What's the mystery?' he asked. 'A picnic is a picnic.'

'Absolutely. Now, go!'

Through the dusty cabin windows, she watched him limp along the wharf, then flew at the work which lay in front of her. Meanwhile, Mike stopped to chat with his next-door neighbour, a keen gardener. When he returned, face clean, hair still damp, in a fresh shirt and fresh jeans, he held one hand behind his back. He ducked carefully down into the cabin and came down the steps. Then looked up.

As he did, the music started — haunting Romany music, played on violins. He gaped: the table was set, as if for a feast, with an opened bottle of wine and shining crystal glasses. Clean place mats shone, and silver cutlery glinted. At each end of the cabin table, candlesticks stood and the candles burned, their fragrance overlaying the smell of new wood from the cabin doors.

'Not quite finished,' Becky said. 'The food's due, any moment. Would you like a glass of wine — specially borrowed from Noel's fairy stock?'

'Yes, please,' said Mike.

The boat rocked, as a waiter from the canal-side pub brought down their takeaway in polystyrene boxes. 'Enjoy!' he said, and left.

'Sit down,' ordered Becky. From her plastic bags, she brought out shining dinner plates, and opened the takeaway boxes. The mouth-watering smell of fish and chips filled the cabin. She dished them up neatly. 'Not yet,' she warned, reaching into the bag again and bringing out a vinegar bottle and a salt cellar. She set these neatly on the table.

'That's it,' she said. 'I think I've remembered everything . . . the wine, the candles, the gypsy music, the fish and chips, and the salt and vinegar. But no pickled onions.

There's only one thing missing . . . don't tell me . . . I'll remember.'

She clicked her fingers a couple of times, then feigned recollection. 'Somebody has to get down on one knee — his good one.'

'And?' said Mike, a quiet smile on his face.

'I think what he says begins with *W* and finishes with *ill you marry me*. Or something like that. But I'm not too sure. And he might have changed his mind.'

'He might just,' agreed Mike.

'In which case I pack up the fish suppers and take them back to Noel . . . '

'Waste of good food,' objected Mike. 'They would be cold by then.'

'It is an hour until the next bus home,' agreed Becky.

'Can he eat his fish supper, while he's thinking?'

'No,' said Becky. 'It's ask, or starve.'

'Oh well,' sighed Mike. He rose and brought out the hand he'd been holding behind his back. It held a solitary red rose, in the full glory of its bloom. He bowed, and presented to it her. 'I got this from my neighbour's garden, so it's probably full of caterpillars,' he said.

He went down on one knee, as promised, looked up, and asked — his eyes twinkling. 'What was it I had to say again?'

'Don't you dare!' she warned.

Mike's smile faded, and the laughter in his eyes was replaced by a huge tenderness. 'Becky Calderwood,' he said quietly. 'I think I fell in love with you, from as far back as that Saturday morning in Ormskirk. I love you truly, madly, deeply, and I want to marry you. Will you please be my wife?'

Becky sniffed the flower, savouring the moment. 'The *truly, madly* bit has been used before,' she complained.

'But it was a good film.'

'Absolutely. So my reply is this. Mike Preston — I love you and I trust you with all my heart. Yes, I accept. And I pray that I will be your wife until the day I die.' She paused. 'Mike, these words about loving and trusting were always far more difficult to say, than 'I do.' But I can say them now, without hesitating for a second. And mean them, with all my heart.'

Mike rose from the floor, and gathered her into his arms.

'Love you, Becky,' he said gently.

'Love you too,' she whispered back.

★　★　★

Noel sat in the stern well of the *Ella Mae*, shivering. 'It's too early in the year, to be sitting out like this,' he grumbled.

'Don't be such a grump,' said Henrietta.

'It's my boat,' he argued. 'I can be as big a grump as I want. I'm the captain. My word is law.'

'Fiddlesticks,' said Henrietta. 'You'll do as you're told.'

'All right,' said Noel. 'Isn't it good to have everybody together again — the babies too. Look at them, walking back from the village like a Sunday School outing.'

Two family groups meandered along the path, the two men heads-down and deep in talk, Becky and Kathy with the babies in their arms, and the two older children out in front, running.

Noel smiled. 'I'm coming over all avuncular,' he said.

'Is it catching?'

'Probably.' Noel lifted a hand to shade his eyes, then found himself wiping the tear flowing down his cheek. 'Damn,' he said. 'I'm supposed to be a crusty, hard-nosed old journalist. No illusions left.'

Henrietta smiled gently. This quiet man had woven himself round and through her heart, like an old country rose bush, growing until he'd filled all the spaces that had ached in her life.

'It would be a sad existence, without

illusions,' she said.

Noel looked up, smiling. 'Illusions, and one certainty,' he said.

'Which is?'

'That it's not just your old school that is blessed. Every life it has touched has been transformed. Made happy.'

'Mine too,' she said quietly. 'What are they going to say, when you tell them?'

'Me? That's your job!'

'It was your idea.'

He sighed. 'OK, we tell them together.'

So they sat and waited for the young folk to come. To meet — and to congratulate — the two oldest newly-weds in Britain.